THE LAWYER

A GRUMPY/SUNSHINE MC ROMANCE

NICHOLE ROSE

Nichole Rose

CONTENTS

Dedication — 1

About the Book — 2

Chapter One — 4

Chapter Two — 14

Chapter Three — 25

Chapter Four — 40

Chapter Five — 52

Chapter Six — 67

Chapter Seven — 85

Epilogue — 94

Author's Note — 107

Silver Spoon MC — 108

Instalove Book Club — 110

Beach House Beauty — 111

Follow Nichole — 115

More By Nichole Rose — 117

DEDICATION

To BOM – Thank you for being my biggest supporter, my most fiercest protector, and the greatest man I've ever known. My joy will always be you.

About the Book

Something about this grumpy lawyer fits this sunshiny runaway just right...

Jude "Fifth" Despora

Someone has been sleeping in my bed...only it isn't me.

And I didn't give her permission.

But when I finally come face to face with my little intruder, she knocks my world out of orbit.

Devin Arakas is the sweetest little treat I've ever seen.

I look at her and ache to be her daddy.

But I'm a lawyer, and she's off-limits.

Until I find out why she's hiding in my bed.

No one is taking her against her will.

Not her brother. Not her uncle. No one.

Not unless they plan to go through me and my MC.

Devin Arakas

I grew up in the biggest crime family in Texas.

I love them like crazy, but I'm not ready to go back to Houston.

Silver Spoon Falls is where I belong.

So when my brother and uncle show up to take me home...I run.

I didn't mean to get caught in Jude Despora's bed.

But I don't want to leave it either.

Something about the overprotective, gruff lawyer fits me just right.

He says he can't have me, but he can't keep his hands off me either.

No one makes my heart sing the way he does.

This man was meant to be my daddy.

But will he really fight my family for me, or is my fairytale destined to end in heartbreak?

Chapter One

Jude

"**W**ho the fuck has been sleeping in my bed?" I growl, stomping into the living room of the Silver Spoon MC clubhouse where my brothers are gathered, preparing for a run. I was supposed to go with them, but that's not happening. I've been in Houston all week with Adam and Fischer, two new lawyers at my firm. We're trying to convince a pain in the ass judge to release one of my clients. She's a single mom with a special needs daughter. Holding her until trial is fucking stupid. She isn't going anywhere. She shouldn't be facing charges in the first place. As far as I'm concerned, she did the world a favor when she shot the asshole abusing her.

"Uh, you?" Declan "Bender" Valentine pushes his dark hair back from his face, looking up from the baby on his lap to smirk at me. "All by your mother-fucking lonesome."

"Fuck you very much for the reminder that we aren't all living in domestic bliss," Cormac "Giant" Carmichael grumbles, scowling at Bender.

"Poor bastards," Andreas "Playboy" Romano says, shoving more shit into his saddlebags.

His wife, Catriona, smacks him on the shoulder, telling him to hush. He just smiles. These days, he's always smiling. His sister is home, and his wife is pregnant. His life is all aces as far as he's concerned.

"I told you I heard something in his room last night, Tate!" Samara cries, smacking our VP on the chest at the exact same time. Women. Swear to God, they communicate every strong belief through their delicate little hands. Usually with a well-aimed smack for emphasis. It's fucking cute as hell. "But you wouldn't listen."

"Baby girl, the only thing you heard in there was a fucking mouse," Hands tells her, trying to ease her mind. Hands is protective of Samara and their baby girl, Scout. Nothing upsets them if he has a say about it. I don't miss the grim look he and Jason "Cash" Montoya, our president, share, though. Something is up.

Fucking great. I was kinda hoping for a break from the bullshit for a while. We've had more than our fair share of that over the last year. Between Playboy's father, a rival MC, Bender's girl being taken hostage, and half the goddamn club falling in love, I've been running flat out all year.

I'm exhausted and irritable as fuck. I haven't even been home in a week. I came straight here when I got back into town an hour ago. Can't a man take a weekend off?

Apparently fucking not.

"Hands, Fifth, help me carry this shit out," Cash orders, nodding at the already packed bags piled in the corner. He could easily carry them himself. Which means he wants to talk.

Fuck my life.

"Yeah," I sigh, stomping forward to grab two of the bags. Hands passes their baby girl to Samara and then drops a kiss on her forehead before grabbing the other two. Scout jabbers at him, flailing her little arms. She's growing like a weed now that she's out of the woods. She doesn't even look like the same dangerously sick baby we met in the hospital six months ago.

We file out of the room behind Cash, headed for the front door.

I squint my eyes against the early morning sunlight, scowling. It's too bright and cheery out for early February. Hell, maybe it's too bright and cheery out for me. I've turned into a crabby motherfucker lately. All work and no play will do that to you. But I have a law firm to run, an MC to protect, and clients like Betty to defend. It doesn't leave a lot of time for anything else.

"Everything go okay in Houston?" Cash asks, leading the way to the row of bikes lined up outside the clubhouse beside his Escalade. The whole club is making a charity poker run to Dallas, wives and babies included. We do it every year to raise money for the pediatric hospital where Hands works. "You get your client out?"

"Not yet. The judge is being a dick," I mutter. "She has a previous assault conviction from ten years ago, so he wants to throw the book at her."

"Prick," Cash grunts.

"I'll get her out eventually." Since opening my own firm, I don't take a lot of cases myself. Those I do are usually like this...domestic violence victims who can't afford decent representation. *Stand Your Ground* doesn't mean much when you're a woman. It certainly doesn't here. This prick claims she shot him for the hell of it. Her bruises tell a different story, but they arrested her on attempted murder charges anyway. The D.A. is willing to let her plead down to aggravated assault, but fuck that. I'm not letting her go to prison for saving her own life.

But Cash didn't call me out here to talk about my case or the criminal justice system.

"What's going on?" I demand, placing the bags on the ground beside the Escalade.

"You sure someone was in your bed?" Hands drops his bags beside Cash's bike—a custom black Ducati Diavel 1260. The bike is an expensive monster. Cash babies the fuck out of it.

"Positive. I don't fucking wear makeup." There were traces of mascara all over my pillow. Considering that I also haven't had a woman in my bed in...fucking ever...well, it doesn't take a rocket scientist to figure it out. I'm not saying I'm a choir boy, because I'm not. I was a teenage boy once upon a time. But I realized quickly that casual sex wasn't for me. Call me old-fashioned or whatever. My fucking point is, someone's been in my bed, and I didn't invite them in.

"Shit," Cash curses.

"Son of a bitch," Hands says at the same time, his face falling into lines of worry. The same reflects in his eyes, the green darker than usual, subdued. "You think it's her?"

"Maybe." Cash rubs a hand down his scruffy chin, staring back toward the clubhouse. "Fuck, maybe."

"Either of you plan to clue me in on who the fuck you're talking about?" I growl.

"Devin."

Devin.

My dick throbs as soon as he says her name. Devin Quartermain has been fucking with my head since the first time I set eyes on her at Petal Pushers—Hadley and Kyra's flower shop. She's a curvy little ball of sunshine with the sweetest smile. The things I want to do to her would shame the devil. They'd probably horrify her. She's eighteen, far too goddamn young for me.

I'm twenty years older than she is. I feel like a sick son of a bitch for even thinking about her the way I do. But I can't seem to help myself either. She's the kind of beautiful that makes a man crazy. Raven hair. Big brown eyes. Olive skin. A mouth I could get lost in. Hips I could sink my hands into. Her sexy little body turns me the fuck on. She haunts my mind.

I feel like a goddamn creep for thinking about bending her over and eating her little holes while she's screaming for daddy. Until the day I met her, the desire to have someone call me daddy never crossed my mind. I never wanted it, never needed it, never even considered it. And then she waltzed into the flower shop like a bright ray of sunshine and annihilated everything I thought I knew about myself, honor, and what's right.

I tell myself I need to stay the fuck away from her and Petal Pushers...but I still find myself making excuses to stop by just to catch a glimpse of her. The lawyers at my firm think I've taken up gardening as a hobby at this point because I bring in so many goddamn flowers.

Yeah, she's fucking with my head. Majorly.

"Why the fuck is Devin sleeping in my bed?" I growl.

"I don't know that it is Devin," Cash says, holding up his hands in a placating gesture. He's a smart son of a bitch. He's the only one of our brothers who realizes that shit has changed for me. I don't think he knows why, but I have a feeling he knows Devin lies at the heart of it. "But she quit Petal Pushers out of the blue last week, and no one has seen her since."

"What the fuck?" I glower at him, my blood pressure rising. Why the fuck didn't he tell me she quit? I want to ask but swallow the question back. I know why he didn't tell me. It's not my fucking business. I made sure of that myself, didn't I? I can't stay away, but I won't get close. I just watch from a distance, stalking her like a fucking creep.

"Rulie and Gloria think someone has been sneaking into the clubhouse at night," Hands says. "Things aren't where they left them, little shit keeps coming up missing. Two days ago, Hadley swore she heard someone crying in the middle of the night when she and Cash were here. Then Samara heard someone moving around in your room last night when we crashed here."

Aside from Rulie and Gloria, none of us live at the clubhouse, but we all have rooms here. We have a rule about not drinking and driving. If we pick up a bottle, we're here until we dry out. Doesn't matter if it's one bottle or five. No one gets on a bike or behind the wheel with alcohol in his system. Besides, as much fucking time as we spend here, having rooms here just makes sense.

"Why aren't the cameras picking this shit up?" I demand. Finn "Hacker" Taylor, our resident computer virtuoso, and Giant have this place wired up tighter than the Pentagon. After everything we've dealt with lately, our security is top-notch. A SEAL platoon couldn't hack through it, let alone one curvy little slip of a girl.

"I had them shut them off," Cash says quietly, leaning back against the Escalade with his arms crossed over his broad chest.

My first instinct is to get pissed. We've been through too much bullshit lately for him to be cavalier with everyone's safety. But this is Cash we're talking about. One thing he isn't is cavalier, especially when it comes to the safety of the people he loves. He'd bleed for our brothers. He'd lay down his life for his wife and kids. If he turned the cameras off, he had a reason. A damn good one. So I take a breath, take a beat, and chill the fuck out.

"Explain," I growl. Okay...so maybe I'm not that fucking chill.

"If it's her, she's hiding here for a reason," he says, giving me a sharp look. He doesn't call me on my attitude though. "I'd rather not scare her off before we find out what that reason is. She's been sneaking in for a week. She hasn't caused any damage, hasn't taken anything more than a little bit of food and a few personal hygiene supplies, and goes out of her way to remain undetected. If she meant us harm, she'd have caused it by now."

Shit. We're on the same team here. He's fucking worried about her too.

"You haven't tried to confront her?"

He hesitates for a long moment and then curses. "Are we still beating around the fucking bush here or not, Fifth? Because, straight up, Hands and I were going to set a trap for her after Hadley heard her crying, but I figured you'd want to be the one to deal with this shit."

"Why me?" I ask, scowling at him and Hands both.

Hands snorts, looking everywhere but at me.

"Lie to yourself if you want, brother," Cash says. "But don't fucking lie to me. We all know you're in love with the girl. It's not our goddamn business so we mind our own. But either you handle this, or we will. We can't have her sneaking in and out of the clubhouse. Hadley and Kyra are worried about her, and it's scaring the hell out of the girls. They're convinced the fucking place is haunted."

"Gloria and Samara were Googling fucking exorcists this morning," Hands says.

"Jesus Christ," I mutter, feeling like they've got my feet to the fire here. Truth is...I don't want anyone else confronting her. If something's wrong, I *need* to be the man who fixes it for her. I won't sleep until I know she's safe. She's mine to protect. But I'm the motherfucker my brothers look to for guidance on right and wrong. I'm the one who keeps them on the straight and narrow. I'm an officer of the courts for fuck's sake. And she's eighteen years old.

If I confront her, help her...I'll claim her as my own. My life will revolve around her. Her wants, her needs, her safety, her pleasure. I'll devote every fucking minute to her and her happiness. My obsession will run free. There will be no stopping it.

And if she isn't ready for that? What then? Will I be strong enough to walk away?

Yes. If it's what she wants, I'll walk away even if it kills me.

"I'll take care of it," I mutter, sealing my fate.

CHAPTER TWO

Devin

"Oh, shoot," I whisper, grabbing for Jude Despora's desk when my foot catches on the edge of the windowsill and I nearly topple face first onto the floor. I gulp a deep breath and then hold it, listening for any hint that anyone else in the clubhouse might have heard me. It's eerily quiet tonight.

Usually, the club is full of bright, happy sounds—teasing and laughter and friendly conversation. Rulie and Gloria, a middle-aged couple who take care of the place, live here. The MC brothers are in and out at all hours. I'm never alone. Most people would probably think that makes it a terrible hiding spot, but not me. I don't like being alone. There is safety in numbers, and there's nowhere in Silver Spoon Falls as safe as this place.

The Silver Spoon MC is full of powerful men. The whole world is at their disposal. This place is a fortress a lot like the one I grew up in...only there are no shady deals or dangerous criminals here. The brothers are genuinely good men, like Jude. He's a freaking criminal defense lawyer. He owns his own law firm and makes millions. But he never charges the clients he personally represents. When he takes a case, he takes it for free.

He's not the only one who does charity work. The brothers are a family, and this place is like a home. It's the last place my uncle and brother will think to look for me. Even if they do, no one knows I'm here, so the brothers won't have to lie for me. As far as everyone knows, I quit my job and left town, headed in search of adventure. The truth is far less glamourous.

A week ago, I quit my job, threw only what I could carry into a suitcase, and fled my great aunt's in the middle of the night. I've been on the run ever since, trying to avoid being carried back to Houston against my will. I don't belong there. I never did.

My family may be deep into the criminal under-world, but all I want is freedom. I'll run for the rest of my life if that's what it takes to avoid going back to the way I lived before. I love my Uncle Dante and my brother, Dimitri, dearly, but I spent my whole life looking through the lenses of their fear. Until they sent me here, I didn't know what it meant to be a normal girl. I didn't understand freedom.

I refuse to give mine up now that I've tasted it.

Once I'm certain no one heard me nearly fall, I pull myself the rest of the way through Jude's window and then slide it closed behind me. I leave the blinds open to allow a little light to trickle into the room, knowing I can't turn on the bedroom light. Thanks to the giant magnolia tree butting up against the side of the clubhouse, it's not much, but it's better than nothing. I'm not even sure if anyone is here tonight, but I'd rather not take a chance. Getting the brothers mixed up in my problems is the last thing I want to do.

That's not why I come here. I tried leaving town the first night, but no matter how hard I tried, I couldn't cross beyond the *Welcome to Silver Spoon Falls* sign. Something drew me here instead. *Jude* drew me here. No one knows it, but I'm madly in love with him. I have been since the first time I set eyes on him almost a year ago. He came to the flower shop to help pick up flowers for Cash and Hadley's wedding and I just...froze.

It was like the entire world stood still when his blue eyes settled on me. An earthquake started in my belly, growing bigger and bigger. By the time it stopped, it had started a tsunami and set off landslides, caving in entire sections of my being. I was Pangaea splitting apart and creating new land masses. The seas rushed in to fill all those empty spaces. When they settled, I was different. I was *his*.

I haven't been able to stop thinking about him since. I know he doesn't feel the same way. How could he? In his eyes, I'm just a kid. But when I think about him, I *ache*. God, I ache so badly. I want him as my own, more than I want air or sunlight or the music that soothes my soul.

So I come here. I sneak through his window. I curl up in his bed and let my mind wander. Sometimes, I pretend that he's touching me. Saying things he shouldn't. He does things he shouldn't. And I love it. Oh god, I love it so much. Other times, he's just cuddling me on his lap or feeding me from his plate. He's taking care of me, and everything in my world is perfect. I feel like a princess...adored and cherished.

It's far better than the reality where he doesn't know I exist, and I've never even been kissed. It's better than sleeping in my car and praying my uncle and brother don't find me. Sleeping in his bed is wrong. I know it is. He'd probably be angry if he knew.

Jude is a certified grump. I've never seen him with anything less than a thunderous scowl on his face.

Every time he looks at me, he glowers like I kicked his puppy. It's intimidating...but I'm not intimidated. Seeing that look on his face makes my clit throb and my panties wet. He's a beautiful beast hiding a heart of gold. My fingers ache to weave their way through his dark hair and trace the sharp planes of his face. I want to know what his full lips taste like and if his perpetual five o'clock shadow tickles.

He's a little over six feet tall with deliciously broad shoulders and a tapered waist. In his business suits, he looks every inch the powerhouse attorney he is. The one time I saw him in a t-shirt and jeans, I couldn't even speak full sentences. The thin white fabric stretched over his defined muscles, leaving nothing to the imagination. He looked so damn good!

"Stop thinking about it," I mumble to myself, heat unfurling in my stomach at the memory. I promised myself I wouldn't touch myself in his bed again. When I did it two nights ago, I felt horribly guilty afterward and cried. Sleeping in his bed is bad enough. Getting myself off to dirty thoughts of him in his bed crosses about sixty lines I probably shouldn't cross. He would probably hate me if he knew.

"Stop thinking about what?" a deep voice rumbles in the dark.

I scream, flinging myself away from him. At least I try to fling myself away. But whoever is in the room with me must be a ninja because they're standing behind me. All I manage to do is fling myself right into his arms.

They close around me and a surge of panic fires through me. My mind short-circuits, fight or flight kicking in. I thrash like a hellcat, trying to get free, but he yanks me up against his chest, easily subduing me. I manage to bring my knee up and slam it into his upper thigh, narrowly missing his groin.

"Fuck," he growls, momentarily relaxing his hold on me.

I use that split second to my advantage, yanking one hand free to scratch him.

"Son of a bitch," he snarls, grabbing me again. The next thing I know, I'm on the bed with him on top of me, his weight pressing me into the mattress.

"Let me go!" I cry, tears welling in my eyes as panic threatens to overwhelm me.

"Easy, baby doll," Jude rasps in my ear. "Easy. I'm not going to hurt you."

"J-Jude?" I gasp, every muscle in my body relaxing all at once.

"Yeah. Fucking hell," he swears, rolling off the bed. "Who did you think it was?"

"I...I..." I don't know what I thought. I *wasn't* thinking. "You grabbed me."

"I won't be doing that again," he growls, flipping on the light. "Jesus Christ, Devin."

I blink up at him, my stomach clenching. His white button down is rumpled, the sleeves rolled up. His hair is a mess and he's scowling daggers at me, but he looks gorgeous. Dismay courses through me when I see the scratches across his cheek.

"You climbed through my window," he says.

"I'm sorry." Naturally, I do the least helpful thing possible in this situation. I start crying. I don't even know why! Adrenaline, nerves, shame, fear? A combination of all four? I don't know. But I just assaulted him in his room, which I broke into...and he's a lawyer.

"Are you *crying*?" He sounds horrified. Looks it too.

"N-n-no," I lie, squeezing my eyes closed and then covering them with my hands like that's going to help hide the fact that I'm bawling.

"Jesus. Did I hurt you?" The bed shifts as he sits beside me. A second later, I feel his hands on me, running down my body as he checks me for injuries. His hands are warm and rough, but his touch is gentle. "Did I hurt you, baby doll? I need you to answer me."

"N-no," I whisper.

He expels a breath.

"I hurt you."

"It's a scratch, Devin."

"Are you going to have me arrested?"

He pries my hands from my face. "Look at me."

I shake my head.

"Look at me," he growls.

I reluctantly crack my eyes open to peek up at him.

"You've been sleeping in my bed for the last week." It's not a question or a guess. It's a simple statement of fact. He knows I've been staying here. Oh no.

"Please don't call the police," I cry, scrambling to sit upright as more tears pour down my face. "I p-promise I'll l-leave and not come back. I didn't t-take anything except a few snacks and a toothbrush and deodorant and books to read. I'll pay for e-everything." I try to slide around him off the bed, but he grabs me again, his hands fitting easily around my waist.

"Stop," he commands. "You aren't going any-where."

My shoulders slump, defeat coursing through me in a black cloud of doom. It's over. He's going to call the police, who will call my brother. He'll bribe my way out of jail...and I'll never be allowed to leave Houston again. My freedom will end in handcuffs and humiliation.

I suppose that's fitting since it began in zip-ties and intimidation. Dimitri and Uncle Dante only sent me here to finish high school because one of the cartels tried to kidnap me. My time here was only ever meant to be temporary. But life without the constant threat of violence hanging over my head is addictive. I'm tired of spending my life surrounded by bodyguards, afraid I'll be kidnapped or killed by one of the cartels. I'm tired of being overprotected because of what my family does.

Not that any of that matters now. I'm a criminal too. I have a feeling Dimitri and Uncle Dante won't be very happy to hear about this new addition to my resume. They aren't ashamed of who they are and what they do, but they've always wanted something different for me. The apple still lands in the apple orchard though, right?

"You've been sleeping in my bed for the last week," Jude says again.

"Yes," I admit. There's no point in lying now. I'm already caught.

"Why?"

Okay, maybe there is a point in lying now.

"You weren't using it," I whisper. It's partially true without being anywhere close to the whole truth. Not even the jaws of life could pry that out of me right now. Telling this man that I'm obsessively in love with him is the last thing I want to do. Adding stalking to the list of criminal charges he's going to file against me isn't appealing.

"Devin, baby doll," he growls, losing patience. "Why the fuck have you been sleeping in my bed for the last week? You live with your great aunt."

"I ran away."

That pulls him up short. He blinks those blue, blue eyes at me in consternation.

"I'd rather not drag the MC into this," I say, trying to pull free of his grasp, which only has him pulling me closer. At this point, I'm practically in his lap. He smells like amber and cedar, the base notes in expensive cologne that linger long after he leaves the room. It's an intoxicating combination. One that drives me crazy.

"Too bad," he says, not giving an inch. "Start talking."

"It's just family drama."

"Bullshit."

I huff at him.

"You quit your job, ran away, and have been committing residential burglary for a week straight. That's more than family drama, baby doll," he growls, eyes narrowed on me. "Start talking."

"It's a long story," I hedge.

"I've got time." He seems amused. "It's just me and you."

"It is?" I peer toward the door. "Really? Where is everyone?"

"On a run."

"It's midnight."

"Not that kind of run," he says, and he's definitely amused now.

"I don't understand."

"It's a poker run, baby doll. It's when a bunch of a bikers get together to raise money for charity by playing poker," he explains.

"Oh. And they run?" I try to work out the mechanics, but it seems exhausting to me.

"No, they ride." He chuckles. "There are different stops along the way where they draw cards. At the end, whoever has the best hand wins."

"Cool," I whisper, adding this to the list of things I want to do.

"Stop stalling and start talking, Devin."

"My brother and uncle are in town looking for me. They want to take me back to Houston, but I don't want to go, so I left before they got here. Now, I'm waiting for them to get tired of looking for me and go back to Houston."

"You couldn't just tell them you don't want to go?" He quirks a brow at me.

"You haven't met Dimitri and Uncle Dante," I mutter. "You don't *tell* them anything."

He scowls at this. "No one makes you do anything you don't want to do, Devin."

"It's not that simple."

"Why the fuck not?"

"Because my uncle is Dante Arakas," I whisper.

CHAPTER THREE

Jude

"Say that again," I say, sure I misunderstood.

"Which part?"

I growl at her.

"My uncle is Dante Arakas," she whispers, confirming that I heard her correctly the first time.

"Jesus fucking Christ," I swear, staring at her in shock. The Arakas family is the biggest crime family in Houston, if not Texas. They're virtually untouchable. The FBI has been trying to build a case against them for years, but it mysteriously falls apart every single time. I have my suspicions that has to do with the fact that they're one of the only things keeping the cartels in check.

If not for them, drug and human trafficking through Texas would be a whole hell of a lot worse. And it's not great to begin with. Not saying I agree with the shit Devin's family does, but when the system is broken, sometimes street rules are the only rules that matter. The Arakas family does what the system can't. Cartels actually respect Dante Arakas. They fear him.

Fear is a powerful motivator. It's damn sure an effective one.

I may be a hard ass when it comes to keeping my brothers on the straight and narrow, but I'm a realist too. Light doesn't exist when darkness dies. Rather, light exists relative to darkness. Without it, there is no light. If we never know sorrow, how do we understand joy? If we never know the struggle; how do we appreciate our blessings?

We're human. We clawed our way out of the dirt and fought our way to the top of the food chain. Those instincts didn't just die because we donned fancy fucking suits and learned to fly planes. There will always be crime. Guys like Dante Arakas may be part of the problem, but they aren't the biggest part of the problem, not by far. He isn't selling kids into slavery or murdering entire families just because he fucking can.

I'll take him over some of those shady motherfuckers any day.

"You're a Quartermain," I say.

"I'm an Arakas," Devin says. "My mom was a Quartermain. I started using her last name when Uncle Dante and Dimitri sent me here. They thought it would be safer for me."

"Dimitri?"

"Dimitri Arakas." The tip of her pink tongue peeps out, wetting her bottom lip. "My brother."

"Jesus," I mutter, trying to wrap my head around this. Devin is an Arakas. I release my grip on her to scrub my hands down my face, pretty fucking certain Cash doesn't have a clue about any of this. He would have called us to Church months ago if he'd known. She worked at his wife's flower shop for months with Hadley and Kyra. I'm guessing he never ran her background. Probably thought it wasn't necessary since she was still in high school at the time and living with Beverly Quartermain, who has lived in Silver Spoon Falls since before Jesus was crucified.

"If you'll just let me go, I promise I won't come back," she whispers, wringing her hands together. The misery in her voice cracks my heart wide open. Poor princess is all worked up and out of sorts. She's lost her mind if she thinks I'm letting her leave, though.

She's not going anywhere. Especially not if Dante Arakas is trying to drag her back to Houston against her will. It'll be a cold day in hell before I allow that to happen. She isn't mine—goddamn, I wish she were—but she isn't property either. No one tells her what she can and cannot do and where she will and will not live, not while I have the breath in my lungs to stop it.

"You aren't going anywhere, Devin," I growl, dropping my hands to glare at her.

"Jail?" Her bottom lip quivers.

For someone who grew up surrounded by criminals, she seems awfully terrified of the prospect. Poor princess. Who knows what she's seen in her life? What she's been through? My fucking *soul* cries out in rage at the possibilities. If anyone hurt her, I'll tear their goddamn throats out. They won't ever get near her again.

"You aren't going to jail. You aren't going anywhere."

Never again. Never again.

I don't say that though. Fuck, she'd probably cower in terror if she knew I wanted to lock her up in this room so no one could ever get close to her again. So I could keep her and her light all to myself. She wouldn't have to worry about her family then. I'd keep her so blissed out that she'd forget she even knew what fear tasted like.

Watch it, old man, I remind myself. *She's not fucking yours.*

"I'm not?" Hope fills her brown eyes to the brim, completely bowling me over. "You aren't going to call the police?"

I silently shake my head, my heart caught in my throat. Jesus God, she's too beautiful for words. My dick throbs, cum leaking into my boxers as she stares up at me like I'm some sort of savior, those bright eyes shining. Right then and there, I decide I'll be whatever she wants me to be if it means she keeps looking at me like this.

I'll crawl through hell to satisfy her. Facing Dante Arakas? No problem.

She squeals and throws herself into my lap. I catch her with my arms around her waist as she flings hers around my shoulders, squeezing me in a tight embrace. All the air rushes from my lungs as her scent annihilates me, shredding every bit of control I possess. Her round ass settles in my lap and I just...snap. Like a piece of wire pulled past the breaking point for far too long.

Her back lands on the bed as I flip us over, pinning her beneath me. One hand tangles in her hair. The other settles on her ass, yanking her flush against me. I don't stop until I feel the heat of her cunt against my aching cock.

"You've been sleeping in my bed," I snarl, looming over her like a wild, dangerous animal. I feel like one right now. The civilized, morally rigid lawyer is nowhere to be found. I'm just...base instinct and pure fuck lust as I stare down into her wide brown eyes. Her cheeks are flushed, her lips parted in shock.

"I...I...yes," she whispers.

Is it my imagination or is she squirming beneath me?

Ah, fuck. She is, isn't she? My baby doll is rubbing her little cunt all over daddy's hard cock.

"Why my bed, Devin?" I demand, not believing for a minute that she chose my room at random. It's the least accessible, hidden by a massive magnolia tree. If you didn't know the window was there, you'd miss it in the light of day. You wouldn't ever find it after dark.

"I...I..."

"Don't lie to me, princess."

She whines low in her throat.

"Why my bed, baby doll?"

"Because it's yours!" she cries. "Because...because I couldn't help it."

Ah, hell. My baby doll has a crush on me. I'm suddenly fifty feet tall and bulletproof. And my fucking cock hurts like hell. Jesus, I've jerked the damn thing raw to thoughts of her for the last eight months, thinking about things certain to send me straight to hell. But my balls ache like a motherfucker right now.

I fall forward, catching my weight on my forearms so I don't crush her beneath me. She's so much smaller than I am, so much more delicate. It'd destroy me if I hurt her. The thought alone feels like acid poured directly into my veins. Knowing I made her cry earlier damn near gave me a heart attack.

"I'm an old bastard compared to you, Devin," I growl, nuzzling my face into her throat. She smells so good. Like ripe strawberries and fresh cream. I flick my tongue out, tasting the pulse hammering beneath her ear. It's going wild for me, pounding like a war drum. "You shouldn't be thinking about me like that."

"Can't help it," she moans, craning her head back to give me more room.

I lick a line down her throat, tugging the top of her t-shirt aside with my teeth to expose her collarbone. The tip of my tongue rests in the dip like it was made to taste that exact spot. Goddamn, she tastes like strawberries and cream everywhere. I nip that bone, dry humping her like a teenager on a first date.

"Tell me, baby doll," I murmur, kissing a trail up her jaw. Her skin is soft as silk. "Did you touch your pussy in my bed?"

"I..."

"Answer me, Devin."

"N-no," she says. Most people have tells. Even those who think they're good liars have little signs that give them away when they're being dishonest. As a lawyer, I'm trained to spot them. Devin doesn't have little signs. Hers are big enough to signal Mars. She averts her gaze, unable to look me in the eye while telling a lie. Her voice trembles. She's lying through her teeth.

"Don't lie to me," I growl, nipping at her ear. "You slipped your hand into your panties right here in my bed and touched your pussy, didn't you?"

"Yes!" she sobs.

Ah, goddamn.

"Did you think about me, princess?" I ask, desperate to know.

Did you think about daddy? Were you taking his cock like a good little princess?

That's what happens in mine. She slips into daddy's bed and lets him have his way. I worship her perfect body and leave her dripping with my cum. And when she's so blissed out, she can't possibly take another drop of pleasure...then I take mine. I carry her to the bathroom and clean her up. I pamper and spoil her.

She's more mine in those moments than ever before, so trusting and open, so vulnerable. Goddamn, if that's not what makes me cum like a freight train every time. The thought of taking care of her. Of being the one responsible for meeting her every need. I want to be the reason the sun rises and sets in her world. It's fucked up. I know it is. But I want it anyway.

"Jude," she whines.

"Tell me," I growl in her ear. "I want to know what you did in my bed, little girl."

"I t-touched myself," she sobs, raking her hands down my back. "I t-t-thought about you! I'm sorry."

"Are you?"

"No," she hiccups.

If I weren't so fucking turned on, I'd laugh at the defiant pout in her voice. Instead, I groan, rocking my hips into hers. I shouldn't be touching her like this. I shouldn't be kissing her like this or talking to her like this. But she's sweet enough to tempt a saint and I can't stop now. God help me, I can't stop.

"Kiss me, princess," I breathe. In for a penny, in for a pound, right?

She eagerly tips her face up to mine, a sweet little lamb to the sacrifice.

I seam my lips to hers, somehow finding salvation and damning my soul in the same breath. She's soft and sweet, breathing her breath into my lungs with an excited whimper I feel in my bones. My stomach clenches, my cum spilling into my boxers. They're a mess now, soaked with the evidence of what she does to me.

I sink into her kiss like a man submerging himself in a baptismal font. Calm settles over me, the rest of the world disappearing. For one perfect moment, I know what it means to be perfectly at peace. And then she makes the sweetest little sound of delight and my cock *throbs* with need. Obsession pours through me like liquid fire, annihilating any chance I had of resisting her. It burns to ash in seconds, unable to withstand the power of her kiss.

I growl against her lips, sinking deeper. My hips crash into hers, riding the hard ridge of my dick against her cunt. The bedsprings squeak as I hump her like a fucking dog in heat—pumping, pumping, pumping. I can't stop. I won't. This little princess is mine.

"Jude, Jude," she sobs beneath me, her voice rising like an aria. She moves with me, squirming and wiggling, grinding her pussy against my cock. I don't have to ask to know she's never been touched. I can smell the virginity on her. I can taste it. She's artless, innocent. But she wraps those long legs around my hips and bounces against my dick like she knows exactly how to get herself off using daddy's cock.

"Don't stop, princess," I snarl, dipping my head to lick and bite her tits through her t-shirt. "You grind that pussy on this dick until you come. You'll sleep in wet panties tonight, so you remember the punishment next time you think about lying to me."

She sobs my name again, louder this time. It's not the one I want to hear though. I've already crossed too many lines with her. For a split second, I try to convince myself not to cross this one too. A split second is all that battle with my conscience lasts. This little princess is mine. It's time she knows it too.

"It's Daddy, baby doll," I say, lifting my head to meet her gaze. She's drunk with pleasure, her expression dazed. "That's what you call me when you're grinding on my cock. Daddy."

Her lips part, that pink tongue peeping out. Something in her expression shifts infinitesimally. It's so subtle that I doubt anyone else would have even noticed. But I notice everything about this girl. I always have. She doesn't just like the thought of me being her daddy. She fucking *loves* it.

Ah, hell. There's really no going back now. Not for her...and definitely not for me.

"Yes, daddy," she whispers.

I plunder her mouth, trying to steal her soul and claim it as my own. She already has mine. I gave it up months ago. Right about the time I stepped into Petal Pushers and noticed her for the first time. It's been hers since then. I've just been delaying the inevitable, trying to fight fate. Not for my sake, but for her own.

She deserves more than to be tied to a motherfucker like me. But my life is hers regardless.

"Daddy," she gasps, stiffening beneath me. "I...I'm—"

"Ah, fuck. Are you going to come for daddy, princess?"

"Yes!" she sobs, her nails embedded in my back as she writhes beneath me.

"Do it, princess." I pump and grind and hump her into the fucking mattress, desperate to get her there, to be the reason she falls apart around me. I've always played by the rules and kept my nose clean. There are no rules when it comes to her. None I won't break anyway. To be the man she calls daddy—to be the man who *deserves* to wear that title—for her, I'll do whatever it takes.

"Daddy!" she wails, tilting her head forward. Her face lands against my neck. For a second, I think she's just holding onto me as the orgasm wracks her beautiful body...and then her teeth close on my skin, delivering a sharp bite.

I bellow into the room like a wounded bear. My dick pulses, cum shooting into my boxers as my balls give up the fight. I come all over myself, roaring in triumph as she marks me as hers. I'm not just Jude any longer. I'm Devin's Daddy.

Fuck. I'm her daddy.

"Jesus Christ," I gasp, still rocking my hips against hers, wringing out every ounce of pleasure I can from her. She's shaking beneath me, adorable whimpers falling from her lips. My heart pounds like I just ran a marathon. "You're going to kill me, princess."

"No," she mumbles, tightening her arms around my neck as if she can physically prevent Death from stealing me from her arms. "You aren't allowed."

"Yeah?" I smile for the first time in days. I forgot how sweet she is. For the people she loves, she probably would fight Death himself. She loves fiercely, with a heart as pure as the driven snow. "Says who?"

"Me." She yawns, burying her face in my shoulder. "I'm sleepy, Jude."

I brush my lips across her forehead and then pry myself off her before picking her up and moving her up to the head of the bed. Once I throw the covers back, I pull her shoes off and then her socks. Her toes are painted hot pink. Her chubby feet are fucking adorable. Jesus. Who knew feet could be a turn-on? I press my lips to the top of each one and then work her jeans down her hips, groaning at the sight of her long legs.

Her olive skin and thick thighs have my dick stirring back to life. She's too damn beautiful. There is nothing girlish about her body. Like the statues and carvings of the spiral goddess, a representation of divine feminine power and fertility popular in polytheistic religions, her hips are wide, her belly soft, and her breasts high and firm. She was made for babies and motherhood.

Her little pink panties are soaked with her juices. The scent of her arousal has my mouth watering, the desire to spread her open and gorge myself on her rising like the tide. I fight it back, knowing she needs sleep. She can barely hold her eyes open.

I toss her pants off the side of the bed and crawl up over her, brushing wild strands of hair out of her face. "Lift up, princess," I murmur. "Let me get your bra off."

She grumbles wordlessly, giving me an adorable pout. She sits up though, letting me pull her t-shirt and bra off. Her hard nipples practically beg for attention. Every inch of her is breathtaking. My hands shake as I slip her t-shirt back on over her head, knowing she won't get any rest if I don't. I won't be able to keep my hands off her.

"Now you can sleep," I chuckle, laying her back down in the bed.

She sighs happily, burrowing into my pillow. She doesn't open her eyes the entire time, trusting me to take care of her. My heart pulses, my throat tight as I run a hand down her round cheek. This right here...this is perfection.

Dimitri and Dante Arakas will have to step over my rotting corpse to get their hands on her.

I shift slightly, and she reaches for me.

"No, daddy. Don't go."

I glance down at her, but she's passed out, talking in her sleep.

Huh. Even in her sleep, she wants me to stay.

Even in her sleep, she called me daddy.

No, she's not going back to Houston. She's not going anywhere.

CHAPTER FOUR

Devin

"You're being weird," I whisper, staring at Jude. He's standing across the island from me in the massive kitchen, scowling at nothing. He looks like a pissed-off angel against the backdrop of sunlight flooding in from the windows behind him. Beams of it even dance around his head like a halo of light. He's been scowling ever since I woke up and found him in here this morning. It's starting to stress me out a little bit. When I fell asleep last night, for the first time since my parents died when I was nine, my life felt almost perfect. Like I was living in a fairytale.

Jude kissed me. He called himself my daddy. How many times have I whispered that forbidden word to myself in the dark of night? Too many to count. I never imagined I'd ever say it to him though. I thought if he ever knew how badly I wanted that, he'd flee in the other direction. But he didn't flee. I didn't even bring it up. *He* did.

In that moment, I was on top of the world, soaring fifteen feet off the ground. I was untouchable. Now though...now I'm worried. I think he regrets it. My stomach is all twisted in knots. Anxiety churns through me with every beat of my heart. I don't like it.

I want to go back to last night. I won't fall asleep this time. I'll stay awake and savor the moment so it doesn't end. Maybe we'll do more this time. He'll touch me, or I'll touch him. Anything to prolong the joy and stave off this, this...gnawing worry.

I don't want him to regret me.

"Did you sleep well, Devin?"

We're back to that this morning too. Devin. Last night, I was his princess. I was his baby doll. Today, I'm Devin. My mama named me after her favorite person in the world—my dad. I've always loved my name. Not today.

"Yes." I push my plate away. It's the first home-cooked meal I've had in a week. Jude cooked it for me. My plate is overflowing with bacon and eggs and hashbrowns and toast. Way more food than I could eat in a week. But I'm not very hungry.

"You need to eat," he says, frowning. He's always frowning. At me, anyway. I know he smiles at his brothers. I've seen him. I've heard him laugh and joke with them too. But he's always grumpy with me. He's a grumpy daddy bear. Except...maybe he doesn't want to be?

More anxiety churns through me.

"I'm not hungry."

"You've been living on protein bars and crackers."

"I had food."

His scowl deepens. "Protein bars, a box of crackers, a couple of purloined bananas, a piece of cake, a half box of oatmeal pies, and two hot dogs isn't food, Devin."

"You know what I took?" I ask, nonplussed. I didn't expect that. Honestly, I didn't think anyone would notice. They keep this place fully stocked. Not that that excuses me for stealing. It was still wrong. "I'll pay the MC back for what I took. I just don't have any money right now."

"Why don't you have money? You've been working at the flower shop for a year."

"It's in the bank," I whisper, dropping my gaze to my hands. "I was afraid if I used my card, Dimitri would be able to track me. He's good at that kind of stuff."

Jude grunts.

"I'll pay you guys back, I promise."

"We don't want your money, Devin."

"Oh." I swallow. "Um, what do you want?"

"Right now? For you to eat your breakfast."

"I'm not hungry."

He sighs and sets his coffee mug down on the island before stomping around to my side. His steps actually vibrate the floor. He's not in a suit today. He's in faded jeans and a black Henley. He looks so damn hot. The flesh between my thighs pulses every time I look at him. I've been squeezing my legs together all morning, but it's not helping at all.

He stops beside my stool and hooks a foot around the bottom, dragging me toward him. The stool screeches across the porcelain tile, probably scratching it all up. Ms. Gloria won't be happy about that. He should really be more careful and not make more work for her. I'm not telling him that though. He's grumpy enough already.

"Up," he demands, placing his hands around my waist and then hauling me out of the seat. He places me on the island beside my plate and then settles into my seat. He's so much taller than I am that we're nearly eye to eye.

"What are you doing?"

"Feeding you," he growls, painstakingly cutting off a bite of egg.

"I'm not hungry."

"Yes, you are."

"No, I'm not."

"Baby doll, stop being stubborn."

"Then stop making me sad!" I cry.

His eyes widen, genuine shock filtering across his face.

"That's the first time you called me baby doll all morning," I whisper, avoiding his gaze. "You're being grumpy again and weird. I don't like it. If you regret last night, just tell me. I'm a big girl. I can handle it. But don't just shut me out and expect me to take the hint, Jude. That's rude and it's making me sad."

"What the fuck?" The fork clatters against the plate. "Look at me, Devin."

"Are you just going to scowl at me again?"

"Look at me."

"Fine!" I throw my hands up in the air and reluctantly shift my gaze back to his. And oh boy, he's *really* scowling now. His face is thunderous.

"The only thing I regret is the fact that you aren't dripping my cum and screaming for daddy right now, princess," he growls, his voice so deep it sends chills through me.

My nipples immediately harden, my clit pulsing. I can't squeeze my legs together this time, though. He's sitting partially between them, preventing me from finding the friction I now desperately need.

"I'm not shutting you out, either. I was trying to give you time to wake up before I put my greedy hands all over your pristine little body. And I'm a grumpy motherfucker because I should be touching you every goddamn minute of the day and I'm not," he growls, rising to his feet. "That's a fucking problem for me."

"Oh," I whisper.

"Yeah. *Oh*."

He looms close, his face inches from mine. "If you want to be daddy's little princess all day, every day, say the word," he says quietly. "I'll rip my own heart out before I tell you no, Devin."

"Jude," I whisper.

"That's not my name."

"Daddy."

"You deserve better than me, princess." He groans, resting his forehead against mine. "I'm a dirty old bastard for the things I want to do to you."

"L-like what?"

He groans again. "You're killing me here."

"Yeah?" I smile, pleased by this revelation. I like the thought of unraveling him. He's always so put together, so unruffled. This side of him is so raw and unrefined. It's so *sexy*. Jude is a fiercely intelligent, wealthy, powerful man. Standing in his presence is like standing in the sun. It's scorching hot and bright enough to burn. But my daddy? He's an unruly, untamed beast. Standing in front of him is like standing on the surface of the sun and realizing it was made just for you. It's pure light, pure power. And god, it's incredible.

"You aren't going to behave, are you, princess?"

"I plead the fifth."

He smiles, his eyes crinkling at the corners as devilish amusement overtakes his expression. "That's my line." He says it all the time. Usually when the brothers ask him something he doesn't want to answer.

"Just trying it out."

"I'll make you a deal," he offers.

"Oh, a deal with a fancy defense lawyer?" I tease, tapping my bottom lip.

He narrows his eyes at me, making me giggle. "Eat your breakfast while we talk, and then you can misbehave all you want when we get back to my room."

"Pinky promise?" I hold my pinky up.

He eyes it curiously for a moment as if unsure what to do and then hooks his pinky through it. "Pinky promise," he says.

"Okay," I agree and then fidget. "But, um, what do you want to talk about?"

"Why you're running from your family."

I sigh heavily, my shoulders drooping.

"Did they hurt you, baby doll?" he asks, danger glinting in his blue eyes.

"No, of course not," I hurry to say. Guilt pricks at my heart. I love my brother and my uncle so much.

I don't want Jude to think badly of them. "Dimitri was barely out of college when our parents died. But he and Uncle Dante made sure I never wanted for anything. They spoiled me."

"Then why are you running, princess?" Jude asks, picking up my plate again. He scoops up a big bite of egg onto the fork and holds it out to me.

I obediently take the bite, chew, and then swallow before answering. "Because the one thing they couldn't ever give me was freedom," I say. "People...bad people...don't like them. For reasons." I chew on my bottom lip, hesitant to admit that my brother and uncle basically run the criminal underworld in Houston. I'm sure Jude probably figured that out himself when I told him who I am but saying it out loud is different. I may not want to go back home, but I don't want to see my family suffer either. I don't want to pit the three men I love most in the world against one another.

Jude isn't like my brother. He isn't like Uncle Dante. His moral compass isn't a pendulum that swings depending on the situation. He does what *is* right because it's what's right. He fights for good because it's good. My brother and my uncle...well, they do what *they* believe is right, even if they have to do wrong to do it. Their definition of right and Jude's are vastly different. They aren't evil men. They aren't bad men. But they aren't soldiers of the light either. They're just men. Jude, though? He's a soldier of the light.

"Reasons like the fact that your uncle is a criminal kingpin," Jude states, cutting off another bite of egg. "Their enemies targeted you?"

I take the bite before answering. "My whole life, I've been one wrong move from ending up in the hands of their enemies. The summer before my senior year, one of the cartels got too close for comfort. I was tied up in the back of a van when Dimitri's best friend, Constantine, found me," I whisper, shivering at the memory. If he hadn't gotten there in time, God only knows where I would have ended up. I try not to think about it.

"Jesus," Jude breathes, shifting as if he intends to use his body to shield me from the memory. "I'm sorry, princess."

"Me too." I clear my throat and shake off the memory, refusing to dwell on it. It was a long time ago now and I'm safe. "It shook Dimitri up. He and Uncle Dante didn't want to risk the same thing happening again, so they sent me here. I was only supposed to be here until they dealt with the cartel responsible, but I fell in love with Silver Spoon Falls. I fell in love with being free."

"You've never had that before, have you?" he asks.

I shake my head. "I've been guarded my whole life. Here, I can go places by myself. I can have a job and friends and a *life*. I don't have to look over my shoulder every single day. I'm tired of being a prisoner in my own life, Jude. If I go back, that's what I'm going back to. And I know they mean well. I *love* them for loving me enough to want to keep me safe. But that isn't a life. That isn't living. Besides..." I trail off, not sure I'm ready to admit that I don't want to go back because he isn't there.

Is it too soon for that? It feels like we've been *this* forever, but in reality, it hasn't even been a full day. My heart has known him for eight months, but the rest of me is just catching up. Maybe I should let it catch up before I admit that I've been putting off returning because I'm obsessed with him.

"Besides what?" he asks, his eyes shifting across my face.

Maybe that's what I should do...but it's not what I'm going to do. He wants to be all over me every minute of the day. That means something. Maybe he doesn't feel the same way I do, but he feels *something*.

"You're here," I say shyly, staring at my lap.

"Fuck," he rumbles, setting my plate aside. It thumps on the counter. "Am I the reason you didn't flee town, baby doll?"

I nod, still focused on my lap. There's a loose stitch in the hem of my t-shirt where it rests against my right thigh. "I tried to drive out of town," I whisper. "I made it all the way to the Silver Spoon Falls sign, but then I couldn't go any farther." I swallow nervously. "I came here instead. I...I waited until all the lights went off and I slipped in through your window."

"How'd you know what window was mine, princess?" he growls, placing his hands on my thighs. I jump, startled at the sudden contact. He's not finished though. He pushes my t-shirt up to my hips, exposing my panties. "How did you know which window to climb through to get into daddy's bed?"

"I...don't know."

"Princess."

"I memorized it."

"Remember sleeping in your wet panties when you lied to me last night?" He runs his thumb across the seam of my panties, making me whimper. "Good girls don't lie, princess."

"Daddy."

"Tell me." He touches me again and I writhe on the countertop. Oh god, this torture is exquisite. The pressure is just hard enough for me to feel it, but not nearly hard enough to give me what I need. He does it again and then again. Until I sob in frustration.

"I've done it before!" I cry, my head thrown back as tremors wrack my body. "I crawled in through your window and slept in your bed when you weren't here." He lives in a gated community on the opposite side of town. Sometimes, when he's there,

I come here. I can't help it. I need to be close to him. It's like a compulsion I can't resist.

"How many times?" he growls.

"Once."

He touches me again. Punishes me again.

"Daddy!"

"Tell me the truth, princess."

"T-three times." The lock on his window is broken. I should have told someone, but I didn't want anyone to know what I was doing. I didn't want anyone to stop me. So I kept my secret. I kept the one way I could be close to him. And I'm not sorry for it. I should be. If I were a good girl, I would be. But I'm not.

"Oh, princess," he breathes, moving my panties to the side and pressing his thumb to my clit. "You've needed daddy for a long time, haven't you?"

"So bad," I sob, tears welling in my eyes. "I've needed you s-so bad."

"Not anymore, baby doll," he vows, pressing his lips to mine. "Not ever again."

CHAPTER FIVE

Jude

Months. Fucking *months* she's needed me. She's ached for me, hurt for me, and I've let her down. I've made her sad. I've left her sneaking around in the dark and climbing through my window just to feel close to me. If ever I needed proof that I am, in fact, an asshole, it's staring me in the face. My princess needed me, and I couldn't get past my own shit to see it.

I was right about one thing. She deserves better than me. I don't deserve the right to call myself her daddy. Not yet. But I'm going to work like a fucking dog to earn it. My princess won't ever be sad over me again. Fuck that. It doesn't matter what anyone else thinks. All that matters—the *only* thing that matters—is what she thinks, what she needs.

And she needs me to get my head out of my ass and *earn* her.

I scoop her up into my arms, cradling her to my chest as I storm through the clubhouse, headed back toward my room. Cash and Hands will be back later today. I called them this morning. As expected, Cash didn't have a fucking clue about Devin's actual identity. He was shocked. I expected him to have a bitch fit about me claiming her—he has an entire MC and a family to think about—now that we know who she is, but he was shockingly chill about it.

As soon as he and Hands get here, we're going to see her uncle. I don't give a fuck who he is or how dangerous he is. Devin is mine now. She isn't going back to Houston with him. He's lost his fucking mind if he thinks it's safer for her there than it is here. I fully intend to ask him about the motherfuckers who put their hands on her. If he hasn't dealt with them already, the MC will.

We may not be outlaws, but we protect what's ours. And make no mistakes about it, Devin is ours. She's been ours since the first time I set foot in Petal Pushers. Cash knew it. Devin knew it. Seems I was the only motherfucker too stupid to accept fate. I was too worried about being too old for her, and I was hurting her the whole time.

The fact is, I *am* too old for her. She *does* deserve better. But I'll bear that cross gladly to spare her a moment of pain. Let anyone try to come between us. Let anyone try to take her from me. They'll unleash a hell they've never seen. She's *MINE.* The only opinion that matters is hers.

I carry her into my bedroom, kicking the door closed behind me. It slams with finality, leaving the last eight months of hesitation where they belong. In the past. Outside of this room. There is no reservation now, nothing holding me back or stopping me from claiming her. She's my little princess, and it's about time she knows just how obsessed her daddy really is.

I lay her out in the center of my bed, growling when she immediately reaches for me, unwilling to be separated from her daddy for even a second. Fuck. She's so goddamn sexy, so beautiful. How did I not know how much she needed me? How did I not see how she looks at me like I hung the fucking moon just for her?

"Daddy," she whines when I pry her hands off me, pressing them gently back to the bed.

"Patience, princess," I croon, letting her go just long enough to rip my shirt off over my head. As soon as I do, her bright eyes darken, dilating. Her cheeks flush, lust overtaking her expression. She squeezes her thighs together, squirming on top of the bed.

Goddamn, I love seeing that look on her face, knowing my body put it there.

"You like looking at daddy, princess?"

"Oh, yes," she whispers. "You're so beautiful."

I chuckle at her earnest expression, popping the button on my jeans. She watches me in rapt fascination, her chest rising and falling with each excited breath. I tug my zipper down, my cock aching for release.

"Have you ever seen a cock before, baby doll?"

She bites her lip, a guilty look filtering across her face. "Not on purpose, daddy," she says.

I scowl at that, instantly pissed.

"I'm sorry!" she cries, covering her face with her hands. "I didn't mean to do it."

I pry her hands away from her face, refusing to let her hide from me. "Explain, princess," I growl. "Who showed you their fucking cock?" I'm going to find them and show them what their dick looks like from the inside. The horny motherfucker, trying to take what doesn't belong to him. Hell no. *Hell no.*

"N-no one," she says. "I, um, Imighthaveseeny-ours?"

That draws me up short. My rage settles, my eyes flickering across her face. She saw my cock? The horribly guilty look on her face says there's far more to this story than she's telling. It doesn't take a rocket scientist to figure out what she isn't saying. My little princess has been naughty.

"You were spying on daddy, weren't you?" I ask.

"I'm sorry!" she cries again. "I didn't mean to do it."

"Is that the truth?"

"No."

Fuck me. Hacker and Giant are going to lose their fucking minds when they realize this perfect little princess has been slipping past all their security measures for months to spy on me and has been doing it completely undetected. Cowboy and Cash aren't going to be thrilled either. She's eighteen, and she's been waltzing onto the property like it's nothing. Because she couldn't stay away from me.

My dick throbs, my balls aching.

"Since you've been spying on daddy, maybe you don't need to see it now," I say.

Her face falls into an adorable pout.

"Maybe I should make you wait to teach you manners."

"No. I'll be good, I promise," she says. "Please. Please."

I pinch one nipple between my thumb and forefinger, making her moan loudly. Christ, I love that sound. I love how responsive she is. She's an innocent little princess, but she responds like daddy's favorite little fucktoy.

"Take it out then, baby doll," I demand, releasing her nipple to drag her shirt up her body. I pull it over her head, quickly removing it. Her little nipples are hard pink pebbles, begging for attention. "Reach in daddy's pants and pull his cock out."

She jumps to obey, eagerly thrusting her hand into my open fly. I growl when she wraps that perfect little hand around my shaft, touching me for the first time. Jesus Christ. She can barely fit her hand around me.

"You're so big, daddy," she breathes, pulling my dick out of my pants.

Cum spills from the head.

She squeals in delight when it drips down her wrist.

I nearly come unglued as she works her hand up and down my shaft, exploring with the tip of her tongue caught between her lips. She looks so fucking cute. Jesus. There's no way I'm going to survive loving this girl. I'm already completely gone for her, and I just keep falling deeper under her spell. Every second I spend with her embeds her more deeply under my skin.

"Enough," I gasp, pulling back when she gets to my balls. My dick falls from her hand, pointing like a divining rod straight at her.

She pouts again, her bottom lip poked out to express her displeasure. I don't let her feel it for long. Before she has time to complain, I kick my jeans off and crawl onto the bed with her, covering her body with mine.

"Oh," she moans, arching beneath me. Her soft curves press to my harder frame, fitting us together like interlocking puzzle pieces. If heaven is real, there's no way it competes with her. It's impossible.

"Kiss me, princess," I demand, brushing my lips against hers.

She offers hers up to me like an obedient little sacrifice, eager to please. I sink into her, getting lost in that sweet mouth. For long moments, we do nothing but kiss. I swear to God, I could drown in her kisses and die happy. She has sugar lips.

When I've had my fill, I break our kiss and work my way down her chest, wrapping my tongue around one hard nipple.

Her back bows off the bed, her little cry of bliss echoing around the room.

Fuck. Playing with her is going to be my new favorite pastime. My whole life, I've been dedicated to my job and the MC. Not anymore. This little princess comes first. Her happiness. Her pleasure. I won't be working at all hours of the day and night anymore unless it's between her thighs, worshipping her perfect body.

I release her nipple and move to the other, dragging it through my teeth.

"Daddy," she sobs, pulling my hair.

I grind my dick against her soft belly, grunting at the pain. I love it. Fuck, I love it. She does too. When I bite her again, she sobs my name and pulls my hair again. She may be a perfect little princess, but she's not delicate. She's not fragile. She was born to fuck.

I work my way down her body, exploring every inch of her with my lips and tongue, leaving my marks all over her so anyone who gets close knows this little princess belongs to her daddy. I want proof of my ownership stamped into her. If that's fucked up, I'll own it. There is nothing soft and sweet about the way I feel for her. It's as primal and possessive as it gets. She is mine. Period.

I'm hers too. Every inch of me. Every breath. Every thought. Every cell. I'm Devin's Daddy. Without her, I'm a shell of a man. I know this because I've been without her for thirty-eight years. I've lived that agony. My life was safe. Boring. A shadow of what it should be. It won't ever be that again.

I kiss my way down her belly and onto her mound, groaning at the smell of her. Her panties are soaked through, her arousal evident. Fuck me. I'm going to gorge myself on this pussy and still want more. I already know it.

"W-what are you doing?" she asks when I nudge her legs apart, fitting myself between them.

"You looked at daddy," I growl. "Daddy's going to look at you. And he's going to use his mouth while he does it."

"Oh," she whispers, squirming beneath me.

"Be a good girl and stay still." I tug her ass toward me, putting her pussy right where I want it. I don't remove her panties yet though. We worked hard to make a mess of them. I intend to enjoy it.

She moans for daddy, gripping fistfuls of the comforter in her hands.

I lean forward, burying my nose in her cunt and breathing her in. Ah, fuck yeah. Strawberries, cream, and virgin pussy. The perfect combination. I flick my tongue out, tasting that wet spot. Her flavor hits my system like a powerful aphrodisiac, instantly addicting me.

I snarl like a wild beast and set to work, cleaning up the mess we made. When I can't taste her anymore, I press harder against her little slit, trying to soak her through her panties. She cries out in ecstasy, her hips lifting from the bed, trying to get closer to my mouth.

Fuck it.

I rip her panties away from her cunt, tearing them from her body.

"Ah, goddamn," I groan, grinding my hips into the mattress. "Look at this little thing." She's bare, her slit coated in her juices. Her swollen clit peeps from between her lips. Cream drips from her little fuckhole, sliding down the crevice of her ass.

I pry her cheeks apart and lick it up.

"Daddy!" she wails into the room.

"Louder, princess," I lift my head to demand. "I want the whole fucking world to hear you screaming for daddy while he takes what belongs to him. Everyone will know who you belong to by the time I'm done."

She wails my name again, louder this time.

"Good girl." I bury my face in her cunt, attacking her like a starving man. I *am* a starving man. I've been starving for her for eight long months. No more. Never again. I splay her legs wide and eat my fill, opening my mouth wide over her little cunt and just...fucking attacking her. I'm not polite about it. I take what I want, eat her how I want, gorging myself on her perfect little princess cunt until she's screaming the walls down around us.

She comes so hard she nearly bucks me off. Her juices squirt out, hitting me in the back of the throat. I roar as the need to fuck her rages through me like an inferno, blazing hotter than the sun. I crawl up over her, yanking her legs up over my hips as I claim her mouth in a hot kiss.

My dick slides through her folds.

She cries out into my mouth, her back bowing off the bed again. Her tits press to my chest, her arms locking around my neck. She's mindless beneath me, drugged and dazed with pleasure. My name falls from her lips in a whimper that's half a plea for more, and half a stunned gasp.

"Hang on tight, princess," I growl, reaching between us to line my cock up at her entrance. "Daddy needs to fuck you."

"Yes, yes," she cries. "Oh, please. Oh, please."

Ah, Jesus. She's killing me and doesn't even know it.

"Now, daddy," she demands. "Get inside me now."

I roar her name, my control in tatters as she begs me to fuck her. Unable to deny her anything, I grit my teeth and rock my hips forward. Her tight little cunt resists for a split second before the head pops in, her walls closing around me. I roar again, jerking my hips forward to impale her on me.

"Oh," she cries.

I fall still, caught in ecstasy, roaring in triumph. Writhing in torment. The need to pound into her is overwhelming. But I can't. I can't. Fuck, I can't. I won't hurt her. Not now. Not ever. I tip my head down, claiming her lips in another kiss, trying to ground myself and give her time to adjust.

She kisses me back eagerly as if she's trying to drown herself in me.

And then I taste her tears.

My soul trembles.

"Baby doll?" I pull back, horrified that I hurt her. My god, what did I do? What did I do?

"You're inside me, daddy," she breathes, tears pouring down her face as she turns those big brown eyes on me. She isn't hurt. *She's happy.* Thank you, God. Thank you. "You're inside me."

"Yeah, princess," I rasp, my throat swelling with emotion. How is it possible to love this girl any more than I already do? Just when I think I've found the depths of my obsession, she proves me wrong, takes me to an entirely new level. "Daddy is inside his princess."

"Am I yours now?" she asks.

Is she mine now? She's always been mine.

"Always," I growl, nipping her bottom lip. "Now, be real good and move with daddy while he fucks his baby into you."

"Daddy," she gasps.

"Don't pretend you don't want it, princess. We both know that's why you've been spying on daddy and sneaking in through his window," I growl. "We both know that's why you let him in that princess pussy without a condom."

She gasps my name again, her inner muscles clenching around my cock.

I pull back half an inch, testing the waters.

"Daddy," she gasps, lifting her hips to draw me back.

"Good girl," I croon. Fuck. She's a vise around my cock, strangling me with her heat. That ripe little princess cunt is going to milk the cum right out of me. I rock into her, fucking her slow and deep, letting her get used to the way it feels to have me inside her. My head kicks back as I revel in the pleasure. It pierces deep, completely annihilating anything I've ever felt before.

This is joy. This is living.

"Daddy," she moans, moving with me, fucking me back. "Oh, daddy."

I pick up the pace, watching her with abject fascination. Every shift of emotion. Every moan. I memorize every single one, claim each one as my own. This little princess is mine. God, she's so fucking mine.

"Harder, daddy," she moans, scraping her nails down my shoulders.

Ah, fuck. There it is.

I give her what she wants, fucking her harder, deeper. My balls meet her ass with a clap of sound with each thrust, earning a cry of ecstasy from her lips each time. I grunt, giving in to the fuck lust. It consumes me. *She* consumes me. We kiss and fuck and touch until I'm lost to her. Still, it's not enough. It'll never fucking be enough.

I flip us, putting her in my lap to bounce her on my cock. She sobs for me, my name leaving her lips in a puff of sound every time I drop her on my cock.

It's still not enough.

"Goddamn, princess," I growl. "Tell me to stop."

"Never stop," she cries. "Never stop."

I flip us again, pounding into her. The bed rattles and shakes. Devin wails for daddy, clawing up my back. Her cunt flutters around my cock.

"Give it to me," I demand. "Come."

She sobs my name. Bites me.

I roar, fucking her without rhythm. Without thought. I'm mindless. Just taking, taking, taking. Her cunt is slick with her juices, welcoming every hard thrust. Her body rises off the bed, arching toward me as if pulled by invisible thread demanding she be as close as possible. Her pussy flutters around my cock again. I tilt her hips up, allowing my cock to drag against her g-spot.

She screams, coming so violently she nearly bucks me off. Her nails make a mess of my back. It's heaven. I groan her name, coming with her, unable to hold it off as her pussy pulses around my shaft, demanding I give it up. I bury my face in her throat, gasping for air, writhing in bliss. Complete.

"Are you okay, baby doll?" I ask, scooping her up into my arms as soon as I can move. I cradle her close to my chest, my heart pounding like a war drum.

"Perfect," she mumbles.

I hold her tightly, my face buried in her hair. It's a curious thing to hold the whole world in your arms and know she belongs to you. It's an honor I'll fight for, bleed for, die for. This little princess...Jesus, this perfect little princess.

I groan and climb to my feet, keeping her cradled in my arms.

"Where are we going?" she asks, her voice thick, sleepy.

"To the tub, princess," I murmur. "Daddy needs to clean you up and take care of you."

"Oh," she sighs happily. "Yay for me."

I smile, handing over another little piece of my heart.

Who am I kidding? The whole fucking thing already belongs to her.

CHAPTER SIX

Devin

"We shouldn't go," I say for the millionth time since Cash and Hands returned yesterday afternoon, chewing worriedly on my bottom lip.

Jude gently pries it from between my teeth, shaking his head. "We aren't hiding, baby doll," he says, his tone firm. "You aren't hiding."

"But–"

"No."

"I don't like this," I whisper, peering out the window at the group of motorcycles bunched up around the SUV like a security escort. Every one of the brothers is out there except Angel and Cowboy, who stayed behind with some of Cowboy's ranchers to keep an eye on the wives and babies. The winged skull on the brothers' cuts blares their allegiance. They don't look like doctors and CEOs and rockstars right now. They look like an MC ready to go to war. For me.

Anxiety churns through me, a parade of conflicting emotions swirling through me. Gratitude, humility, worry, fear. Love. I appreciate them so much for being willing to stand up for me like this, but I don't want anything to happen to them. I don't want anything to happen to Dimitri or Uncle Dante. What if Jude changes his mind and decides I'm too much trouble? Will he really fight for me if Dimitri and Uncle Dante put up a fight?

A thousand different fears run through me at the same time, each vying for attention. Half of them make me feel horribly guilty for doubting Jude when he's given me no reason to doubt him. Those fears aren't the least logical or rooted in reality but they crop up anyway. The other half leave me worried about Jude, the MC, and my family.

I never meant to cause all this trouble.

"Everything is going to be okay," Jude promises, unlatching my seatbelt and pulling me across the backseat into his lap. He wraps his arms around me, holding me tight. "I'm not going to let anything happen to you or to anyone else." He nuzzles his face against my temple. "Trust your daddy, baby doll."

He whispers it in my ear, making sure Cash, who is in the driver's seat, doesn't overhear. I'm pretty sure he and Hands both heard me calling him daddy yesterday. They got back into town while we were still...well, they probably heard a lot of things they shouldn't have heard. I couldn't even look them in the eyes when Jude finally dragged me out of the bedroom last night to talk to them. But they didn't bring it up. They didn't treat me any different.

Jude promised me that they never will. He said that what happens between us is our business and that his brothers will never judge me, shame me, or look at me differently because of it. And then he said that I can call him daddy any damn time I please, and if anyone has a problem with it, they can come to find him.

It was a long time before we said anything else after that. I basically tackled him to the bed. He taught me how to ride his face and suck his cock at the same time. At least he tried to teach me. He didn't last five minutes before he had me facedown beneath him, grunting in my ear about breeding daddy's good little princess again. It was awesome!

I think I want to keep the daddy thing just to myself though. I like having a piece of him that I don't have to share with anyone else. It's meant just for us. In private, he can be my unruly, wicked daddy and I'll be his perfect princess. But to the rest of the world, we can still be Jude and Devin. Or a version of ourselves anyway. I don't think I can pretend that I'm not wildly obsessed with him anymore. I did that for eight months and it was so exhausting! I don't want to try anymore. I want to be madly in love, and I want the whole world to know it.

I want to choose him, and I want him to choose me. I want him to hold me and take care of me and not be able to keep his hands off me like he is right now. If we have to hide that, it's going to break my heart. I *need* this, so damn badly. He anchors me.

"Promise everything is going to be okay?" I demand, holding my pinky up.

"I'll make it okay," he vows, hooking his through mine. He doesn't let it go, though. He brings it to his lips, brushing a kiss across my knuckle. "You aren't leaving with them, baby doll."

"Okay," I whisper.

He holds me for several minutes.

Cash meets my gaze in the rearview mirror, giving me a small smile. I like him. He's so in love with Hadley, my former boss. He said I could have my job back if I want it, and that Hadley and Kyra miss me. He's always been so nice to me. He reminds me a lot of my brother. He's incredibly protective of the people he loves.

"Thank you," I whisper to him.

He gives me a chin lift and then shifts his gaze back to the road.

I rest my head against Jude's shoulder, staring out the window. His brothers ride in tight lines on either side of the SUV, not deviating an inch. They all look so somber and serious. Even Giant, who always looks like he's up to no good, is subdued.

"Are they afraid?" I ask, worried.

Cash and Jude both chuckle.

"Sweetheart, the only thing these motherfuckers are afraid of is walking on Gloria's freshly mopped floor," Cash says, a smile in his voice.

"He's not lying," Jude says, rubbing my back. "This is living for them. We're stuck behind desks or piled up with fucking responsibility all day, every day. But this is the shit we live for...protecting the people who need it, defending what belongs to us. This is who we are, baby doll. This is what life is about."

"Oh," I whisper. "I don't want anyone to get hurt."

"No one is going to get hurt." Jude presses a reassuring kiss to my crown. "We're not going to wage war. We're going to talk and that's all we're going to do. Your uncle is a reasonable man, baby doll. We're going to make him see reason. That's it."

"I still don't like it," I mumble, just so we're clear on that point. Uncle Dante is reasonable. But he doesn't like to be threatened. And Jude the lawyer may be levelheaded...but Jude my daddy is an entirely different matter altogether. We need Jude the lawyer today, but I have a feeling he's going to take a backseat as soon as Dimitri and Uncle Dante start talking about taking me back to Houston. Jude my daddy will step into the ring to stake his claim, and who knows how that's going to go over? He won't be nice and polite and reasonable; I know that much.

"That's because you'd cut out your own heart to spare the people who matter to you even a second of pain, princess," Jude whispers in my ear. "You're selfless and gentle, and you love fiercely. Your heart is pure and so are you. You're a perfect little ball of sunshine."

"Jude," I whisper.

"You're daddy's little ball of sunshine." He slips his hand between my legs, cupping my center. "And this right here? This is how daddy rewards you for it, baby doll."

"Daddy," I moan quietly, my whole body going lax in his arms. My whole body is deliciously sore today. Jude has made me bathe twice and take Tylenol a couple of times. He's so protective. I don't mind the sore muscles though. They're a reminder of what we've done. And what I desperately want to do again.

"Daddy's claiming it again tonight, princess," he growls, his voice pitched low so Cash doesn't over-hear. "He's not stopping until you're pregnant."

I bite my lip, fighting back a loud moan. My whole body bursts into flames, arousal instantly flooding my panties. I squeeze my thighs together, trapping his hand against my center, trying to ride my hips against it. He grunts and grinds his palm into me, biting my neck at the same time.

"Tonight," he says, breathing hard.

I nod frantically, already unsure how I'm supposed to make it until then when I need him so bad right here and right now. I think he broke me. He touched me and turned me into a greedy, desperate princess. All I can think about now is him and getting him inside me again. About him touching me and kissing me and eating me and fucking me. He calls me his good little princess, but I think I might be bad. Gluttony is a sin, isn't it?

"We're pulling in," Cash says from the driver's seat.

My heart stops.

Jude grinds his palm against my center one more time and then reluctantly pries his hand from between my legs. His lips touch the side of my neck in a gentle, reassuring kiss. "Breathe, baby doll," he whispers. "Everything is going to be okay."

Petal Pushers is a small, old-fashioned shop with a small parking lot and big front windows. When we pull into the lot, a black SUV is already parked near the doors. My heart catches in my throat when I see Dimitri, Uncle Dante, and Constantine standing beside the SUV.

Uncle Dante is dressed in his customary dark suit and tie, his expensive Italian leather shoes shining in the sunlight. He's big and imposing. Dimitri is the same size, though there is no getting my brother into a suit. He watches us approach like a hawk, his dark eyes narrowed, his lips compressed in a thin, disapproving line. He's not very happy with me right now.

Constantine is the only one of the three who doesn't look grumpy. He's also the one of the three I'm most worried to see here. They call him the Grim Reaper. He's the man they call when they need something especially dirty handled. He's done things that would make the angels weep. If he's here, it's not good.

"That's Uncle Dante," I whisper, pointing him out to Jude. "Dimitri is the one scowling at us." I lick my lips, trying to work moisture into my mouth, and then nod at Constantine. "That's Constantine Attias. He's, um, he works for my brother and Uncle Dante. He's like their hitman."

"Jesus Christ," Cash mutters from the front seat.

"Would he hurt you?" Jude asks, his hands tightening on me.

"Never," I say without hesitation. Constantine may be a lot of things, but I trust him with my life.

He *saved* my life. He has a thing about women and children. Uncle Dante and Dimitri do too. They won't go after a woman or a child, no matter the provocation. I don't know if it's because they've spent so many years trying to keep cartels from coming after me or if it's just that they find it morally wrong, but they never target the families of their enemies.

"I want you to stay in the SUV," Jude says anyway.

"No."

"Princess."

"No, Jude." I shake my head, holding firm. "I appreciate you so much for wanting to do this for me, but they'll never just accept your word that this is where I want to be. Unless they hear it from me, they won't give up."

"Fuck," he growls.

"I have to do this," I whisper, cupping his jaw. His stubble scratches my palm. "I thought running away was the answer, but I was wrong. How am I ever supposed to prove that I'm an adult capable of making my own decisions if I'm not even capable of *telling* them that I'm an adult capable of making my own decisions?" I want them to hear from my lips that I'm my own person with my own future and that my future is here with the man I love. They don't have to like it, but they do have to accept it. They'll never do that if I spend the rest of my life running.

I can't claim to be an adult and then make childish decisions that hurt the people I love most. My uncle and my brother gave up so much to raise me. They fought for me and protected me and kept me safe. All they've ever wanted is for me to remain safe. They need to see for themselves that I'm still safe, that I'm happy and healthy, and that this is my choice.

"Fuck," Jude swears, gently grabbing my wrist. "Fine. But hear me now, little girl. They aren't getting their fucking hands on you. They aren't taking you back to Houston. You aren't going anywhere you don't want to go."

"That's the plan," I promise, leaning forward to press my lips to his in a hard kiss. God, I love him so much. He's so hot when he's all bossy and territorial. Maybe it's wrong to love it as much as I do, but I don't care. I *do* love it.

Cash pulls in sideways, taking up three spots, and kills the engine. The brothers line their bikes up around the SUV, forming an upside down *V* with the SUV in the middle. None of them dismount though. They all stay where they are.

"Let's go," Jude growls.

Cash mutters a curse and then climbs from the SUV.

Jude opens the door and then steps out before setting me on my feet. He doesn't let me go, though, not even close. He wraps his arm around me, tucking me up against him like he's a piece of me. Even from here, I can feel the weight of Dimitri's unhappy gaze on us.

My brother is overprotective. If he had his way, I'd never date or fall in love or marry. Men would never exist to me. As far as he's concerned, they can't be trusted with me. But he doesn't know Jude. I think if he did, he'd find that he and Jude are in perfect agreement on that particular subject. As far as Jude is concerned, he's the only man that can be trusted with me. He told me so last night.

Uncle Dante keeps his expression clear, his thoughts carefully obscured behind his dark eyes. He's always been harder to read. He doesn't seem surprised to see Jude's arm around me though. He doesn't seem surprised to see the MC either. I know he and Jude briefly talked via phone this morning. I was there for the conversation. It lasted all of three minutes. I'm guessing my uncle has been on the phone ever since, getting every scrap of intel he could on the MC.

Did he call Constantine here after that conversation?

When we pass Hands, he hops off his bike and joins us, striding across the parking lot at Cash's side. Giant gives me the tiniest smile when we pass him, but his gray eyes are more serious than ever.

I shiver even though it's not particularly cold out. The weak winter sun shines brightly overhead, the rays spilling across the parking lot. Wind rustles through the treetops, singing in counterpoint to the growl of the motorcycles as we step beyond them.

We draw to a stop a few feet from my family.

"Hi, Uncle Dante, hi, Dimitri," I whisper, wringing my hands together. "Hi, Constantine."

"Sweetheart," Uncle Dante says. Even though his expression gives nothing away, he can't hide the worry in his voice. "You doing okay?"

"Yes." I swallow hard, feeling about two inches tall. "I'm sorry I worried you."

"You don't owe him an apology," Jude growls, glaring daggers at my uncle. "He shouldn't have tried to force you to do what you don't want to do."

"Fifth," Cash mutters, cutting his eyes at Jude. "Chill."

Jude ignores him, bristling like a pissed-off, territorial daddy bear. "She ran because she didn't trust you not to force her back to Houston against her will."

"You must be Jude Despora," Uncle Dante says, his tone full of wry amusement.

Dimitri is less amused. He's growling softly, his eyes narrowed on Jude.

Hands and Constantine say nothing, instead standing off to the side. They both look bored, but I'm not blind. I know they're both keeping an eye on each other and everyone else. They have that look about them, limbs long and loose, prepared for a fight. It's interesting, but I never thought of Hands as dangerous until this moment. He's so in love with his wife and baby girl and so gentle with them. Seeing him like this though, I realize that he's every inch the warrior.

"That's me," Jude says to my uncle.

"Which makes you Jason Montoya," Uncle Dante says, looking at Cash.

Cash lifts his chin in a nod.

Uncle Dante glances at Hands, who makes no move to introduce himself, and then back to Jude. "I'm Dante Arakas," he says. "Devin's uncle."

"I know who the fuck you are." His gaze whips like lightning from my uncle to Dimitri. "You're the reason she fled her home in the middle of the night. You're the reason she's spent the last goddamn week living off what scraps she could sneak from our kitchen." He draws himself up to his full height, his expression blistering. "You're the reason she was afraid to ask for help."

Dimitri shifts uneasily.

Not Uncle Dante. Irritation flashes in his eyes. "Considering that you've got your fucking arm around my niece, I suggest you watch your tone when talking to me," he says calmly. "I didn't come here to fight. I came here to talk like civilized adults."

Jude glowers, clenching his jaw so hard his teeth grind together.

"Jude," I whisper, placing my hand on his jaw.

He tilts his head down, meeting my gaze.

"Please," I say quietly, shaking my head. I love him so much for standing up for me, but it's my turn to stand up for myself. With him at my back, I can do it. I can do anything.

His expression softens, the anger in his eyes bleeding away. He lifts his hand, brushing it down the side of my face. The look in his eyes...God, I hope he never stops looking at me like this.

"Jesus fucking Christ," Dimitri mutters, the first thing he's said since we got here.

I startle, turning to look at him.

"This is fucking ridiculous," he says, throwing his hands up. "We didn't come to fucking kidnap you. We aren't dragging you back to Houston by the hair of your head, Devin. We thought you wanted to come back home."

"I *am* home," I whisper vehemently, tears welling in my eyes. "Silver Spoon Falls is my home, Dimitri."

"You live in Houston," he says.

"No, *you* live in Houston. That's home for you and Uncle Dante, but it's never been home to me. My whole life, it's been a prison for me, Dimitri. I was seventeen before I had my first sleepover!" I cry. "I was seventeen before I could go shopping or walk to school without bodyguards. That's not *normal.*" Even before my parents died, that was my life. I've always been more closely guarded than the dang queen of England. I never even realized how messed up that was until I moved here.

"You know we were just doing what was best for you, Dev," Dimitri says, his voice soft.

"I do know that, and I love you both so much for working so hard to keep me safe," I say, swiping at my eyes. "But I know what it's like to be normal now. I know what it's like to have freedom and not have to look over my shoulder every minute of the day. I'm not going back to spending every waking moment living in fear of the cartels. My life is here now."

"You mean your life is with him," Dimitri says, scowling at Jude.

"Who I choose to date is my choice, Dimitri."

"He's too goddamn old for you, Dev."

"Too fucking bad," Jude snaps. "I'm marrying her anyway."

Dimitri and Uncle Dante both blink, taken aback by his announcement. It shocks me too. My heart soars toward the heavens and then plummets toward the ground as worry rushes in. But I don't voice it. Not here. Not now.

"I am marrying him," I say, my voice clear and strong.

"Jesus Christ," Dimitri mutters, staring at us in shock. "You're eighteen!"

"So was mom," I remind him, making him flinch. "Does that mean she somehow loved dad less all those years? No, it doesn't. I made my choice, Dimitri. Can't you just be happy for me?" My voice wobbles at the end. "Can't you just love me anyway?"

"Fuck," he rumbles, stomping toward me. He holds his arms out, waiting for me to untangle myself from Jude to fling myself at his chest. As soon as I do, he wraps me in a bear hug like he has so many times in my life. "I will *always* love you, baby sister. Always."

I sob his name, clinging to him.

"If he's not good to you, I'll bury him where no one will ever find him," he whispers in my ear.

"He's s-s-so good to me," I whisper back, sniffling through my tears.

He sighs heavily, squeezing me tight, and then slowly releases me.

I reluctantly turn to Uncle Dante, not at all sure what to expect. With him, it could go either way. He wants what's best for me, but his idea of what's best for me and mine don't always align. He's stubborn and set in his ways. Once he's made up his mind, changing it is virtually impossible.

He eyes me for a long, silent moment, and then blows out a breath, shaking his head.

"You're just like your mom, kid," he says, holding his arms out for me. I race forward, hugging him just as tightly as I hugged Dimitri. He chuckles and hugs me back. "Love you, kiddo."

"I love you too," I mumble, wiping my face on his shoulder.

He releases me and I hurry back to Jude's side, eager to feel his arms around me too. I've got three grumpy bears in my life, but only one of them fits me just right. This one. My daddy.

"Does this mean you're not going to fight to make me go back to Houston?" I ask Uncle Dante, just to make sure we're all on the same page here.

"About that," he says, cocking his head to the side.

Jude stirs uneasily, a growl rumbling in his chest.

"It looks like Silver Spoon Falls may be home to all of us for a while, Dev," Dimitri says with a sigh. "We have something to take care of here."

"And what, precisely, would that be?" Cash asks.

"Business," Uncle Dante says.

Cash scowls.

I gape at Uncle Dante. "You're *moving* here?"

"Looks like it," he says, rubbing a hand down his face and then eyeing me warily. "Is this okay with you, sweetheart?"

"You promise you aren't going to surround me with bodyguards and interfere with my life?" I ask, worried that's exactly what he's going to do. "Because if that's your plan, you should know that I'm not going to cooperate."

"She doesn't need bodyguards," Jude growls. "We protect our family."

Hands and Cash both nod their agreement.

"I see that," Uncle Dante says drily, his gaze flickering to the brothers still waiting by Cash's SUV. His eyes come back to Jude. "If you keep her safe, I won't interfere. But the first time her safety is jeopardized, you and your club will answer to me."

"That day won't come," Jude growls.

"See to it."

"Agreed," Jude growls.

"Agreed," Cash says.

Jude tilts his head toward mine. "Princess? What do you think?"

"Welcome to Silver Spoon Falls," I say, giving my answer without reservation. The three men I love most in the world all in one place? It's almost a perfect fairytale ending. Besides, I know Jude won't allow Uncle Dante to go back on his word. He's my daddy. He'll do whatever it takes to ensure I'm safe without losing my freedom. That's who he is. It's part of why I love him so damn much.

CHAPTER SEVEN

Jude

"You're being weird," I growl at Devin, watching her intently from across my room. We're back at the clubhouse. I wanted to take her to my place for the night, but Cash convinced me to stick around here for another couple of days, just to make sure everything is copacetic with her uncle before I take her off the property. It's a smart plan.

He cleared everyone else out to give us privacy. I know we're not entirely alone though. Cowboy and Kyra are at the ranch right next door. Rulie and Gloria are bunking with them for the night. I imagine he's got Giant watching the place tonight too.

"Am not," Devin says, flitting from place to place like a little fairy. She's antsy, unable to sit still. I can practically hear the wheels of her mind spinning from here. She's not talking though. It's driving me up the fucking wall. I hate not knowing every thought that crosses her mind.

"You are."

"Am not," she sing-songs, making me smile. She's too fucking cute for words.

I push off from the wall and pace toward her, snagging her around the waist before she can dance out of my reach. "Remember what happens when you lie to daddy, princess?"

She moans softly.

"Daddy likes sleeping with that little cunt wrapped around him," I growl, pulling her flush against me. "Wouldn't you rather do that than sleep in wet, uncomfortable panties?"

"Oh, yes," she breathes, her eyes already dilating. Jesus. She's a vision. How'd I manage to keep my hands off her for eight months? I must have been a saint. No, I wasn't that. I was an idiot. Too worried about what people would think about her to see what was right in front of my face. To see how badly she needed her daddy.

The world is still fresh and new to her. She's tasted freedom and thinks she's safe. I'll never tell her any differently. But I'm not stupid. I know she's not safe simply because she's out of sight. With Dante and Dimitri moving here, she'll have a target on her back again. She'll never know that though. She'll never see it. I won't allow her to spend the rest of her life like she spent the first seventeen years—locked up and living in fear. She's had more than enough of that.

It's my job to eliminate any threat that comes for her. She'll never know about them, never have time to fear them. For the rest of her life, I'll be the thing standing between her and anything that means her harm. Me and my brothers. We'll protect her, just like we protect Hadley, Kyra, Samara, Catriona, and London.

I have a feeling Dante and Dimitri will be around to help. Whatever business drew them here...I doubt it's the legal kind. And I doubt they picked this place at random. If the cartels are involved, I'm guessing they're here because she's here, because they'll never let them close to her again. They almost lost her once. Only a fool would risk her twice. Her uncle and brother are far from fools.

I'm not entirely sold on either of them yet, but it's clear they love her. It's equally as clear she idolizes them. I'll swallow my own fucking tongue before I make her unhappy fighting with them. We'll sing kumbaya around the goddamn campfire if it makes her happy. Whatever it takes to keep her smiling.

That's my priority now. My princess. Her world. What she needs.

"Then be honest, baby doll," I croon, sliding my hand around her throat to crane her head back. Her bright eyes lock on mine as if she's unable to look away. "What's going on in that head of yours?"

"Do you want to marry me because you think you have to marry me?"

"What?"

"You think you're too old for me and that what we do is bad," she whispers. "You think it makes you bad." Her bottom lip quivers. "D-do you really want to marry me, or do you feel like you have to do it because it's the right thing to do?"

I gape at her, shocked by the question. Horrified by the tears swimming in her eyes. My god, she really has no idea, does she? Even though that's my fault, it pisses me off. Maybe it pisses me off *because* it's my fault. Because it's intolerable that this girl doesn't already know that my heart beats for her and her alone. It has since the moment I set eyes on her.

"Arms up," I growl, grabbing the hem of her shirt.

"Jude."

"Arms up, princess."

She huffs and then reluctantly lifts her arms, allowing me to strip her shirt off her. I toss it to the floor and then reach for the clasp on her bra. It's gone in two seconds, stripped off her gorgeous body and tossed on the floor with her shirt. Her pants and panties go next, discarded in a heap where they fall.

When she stands naked in front of me, wearing nothing but my marks and an adorable scowl, I drop to my knees in front of her, worshipping at her feet where I belong. And goddamn, the view from here is phenomenal. Her skin glows in the lamplight, my marks dark blotches that stand in contrast to her perfection.

"Jude," she whispers. "What are you doing?"

"Preparing to beg the woman I love to marry me."

She gasps, the sweetest little sound of surprise.

"I am too old for you, princess," I say, staring up at her in complete adoration. "Compared to you, I'm a fucking dinosaur. You got that part right. But the rest of what you said? You couldn't be more wrong. I tried to stay away from you for eight months because I was afraid *you* would be horrified by the things I wanted from you. I didn't give you enough credit, but you were made for me in every fucking way imaginable." I run my lips up her legs, kissing all over her trembling thighs. "You were made to be daddy's little princess."

"Daddy," she moans.

"The only bad thing about what we do," I growl, gently easing her legs apart with my hands on her thighs. She steps out, widening her stance for me. "Is when we stop." I lean forward, spearing my tongue through her folds. "When I have to stop licking this little princess cunt." I run my tongue in circles around her clit, making her cry out for daddy. "Or this tasty little asshole." I rub my finger over her back entrance. "Or when daddy has to take his dick out of you." I press my thumb to her opening, pushing it inside her.

"Daddy," she sobs, clinging to my shoulders as her knees tremble and shake.

"Nothing daddy does to you is bad, princess," I growl against her pussy. "Nothing I feel for you is bad." I lap at her clit, fingering her tight little hole at the same time. "I'm a goddamn *king* between these legs." I eat her for several moments, driving her higher, higher, higher. "You're the reason my heart beats, baby doll. Since the moment I met you, I've loved you wildly, obsessively. I don't give a fuck if I'm too old for you. You're mine. This little princess cunt belongs to daddy."

"Yes!" she cries. "Oh, yes, daddy."

"You belong to daddy," I growl.

She cries out, coming apart around my fingers. I work her through it, coaxing every last drop from her body, teasing her little clit until she's whimpering, her legs threatening to buckle. And then I scoop her up into my arms, dragging her down into my lap.

She drapes across me like a sweet little blanket, all sweaty and panting for breath.

"I didn't tell your uncle that I'm marrying you because I feel obligated," I murmur into her hair. "I didn't say it in the heat of the moment either. I *need* you to marry me, princess. Until you're tied to me in every way humanly possible, daddy won't rest." I run my nose across her crown, breathing her in. "I need to belong to you, Devin. Marry me, baby doll. Please, let me be your daddy for the rest of your life."

"You already belong to me," she whispers.

"Fuck," I growl, my dick jerking against my zipper. Hearing her stake her claim on me is sexy as hell. I fucking love it. "Lift up."

She obediently lifts her hips, allowing me to reach between us to undo my pants, I pull my cock out, hissing in relief. I'm so fucking hard it hurts. She moans when I line up at her entrance.

"Ride me, princess," I murmur. "Fuck yourself with daddy's cock like a good girl."

She immediately sinks down on me, taking me all the way to the hilt. We moan together, writhing in ecstasy in the middle of the floor. Fucking hell, I can't get enough of her. A lifetime together isn't going to be long enough. I want—*need*—more than that. An eternity, and whatever comes after that. I'll stitch us into one soul, make her a part of me permanently.

"Marry me," I groan, notching my hands at her waist to help lift her up and down my cock. "Marry me, princess."

"Tell me again," she demands.

I don't have to ask to know what she wants to hear. I *know* her. God, I know this girl like I know the back of my hand. She exists on pure love. It runs through her veins instead of blood. It's what feeds her, fuels her, sustains her. And mine is her favorite flavor.

"I love you."

She cries out in ecstasy.

"I love you." I lift her higher, drop her harder. Until I feel like *I'm* flying. "I love you."

"Yes, daddy," she sobs, breaking for me. "Yes, yes, yes."

She breaks me too. Cracks me wide open and sweeps into every crevice remaining in my heart and soul. They light up like the sun, my obsession with her growing, growing, so vast it's overwhelming. And still it's not enough. Still, I want more of her. Until she runs through my veins and I exist purely on her. Her love, her light, her smiles.

I flip her onto her back with a roar, throwing her legs up over my shoulders. And then daddy really goes to work. My hips crash into hers, my balls slapping her ass as I fuck my way into her soul, claiming every inch of her along the way. She screams her pleasure, clawing my arms, begging for more, more.

It's a good thing we have the place to ourselves because my princess is a dirty little girl. She demands everything I have, begging for me to go harder, to fuck her deeper. I bite her nipples, tormenting them with pleasure and pain that only spurs her on. I'm rough with her, rougher than I should be. She loves every damn minute of it.

We come together, her screams of ecstasy echoing around the room. I lose track of everything but her as her cunt locks down on me and *daddy* echoes in the corners. I slump against her, holding my weight off her on my forearms. Even though I'm exhausted, I can't stop touching her, though. I run my hands all over her curvy body, placing worshipful kisses everywhere I can reach.

"I love you," I pant between kisses. "I love you. You did so good. God, princess. Daddy loves you so fucking much."

"Mm," she purrs in that sweet voice that never fails to wreck me. "I love you too, daddy."

My heart overflows, and for the first time in my life, I know true joy. It's this. It's her. And it's fucking perfect.

Epilogue
Devin

Five Years Later

"Shh," I whisper, holding my finger to my lips as my daughter and I stand outside of Jude's window at the clubhouse, preparing to sneak in. He's been in Houston, signing contracts with a nonprofit a former client opened. Five years ago, Betty was charged with attempted murder for shooting her abusive boyfriend. Jude got her off on the charges and her life really turned around. She now runs a nonprofit that helps domestic violence victims find legal representation. Jude's law firm just signed on to represent her clients pro-bono. I'm so freaking proud of him.

Then again, I'm always proud of him. My husband is one of the most amazing men I know. He's selfless and caring and will do whatever it takes to help those who need it. I love him more and more every damn day.

"Shh," Dylan whispers back, giggling.

I fight a smile, shaking my head. She's terrible at sneaking. Then again, she's only four. To her, everything is an adventure meant to be undertaken at top volume. I love seeing the world through her eyes. It's so different than the world I grew up in, and I love that for her and her little brothers. They've never spent a single day knowing fear or what it's like to be locked away from the world.

Jude would never allow that. He is our most fierce protector and our most devoted line of defense. Nothing harms us. Nothing even gets close. I know there have been scares over the years. But he never lets them touch me or our babies. He never lets me stress or worry over them. He just handles them.

I appreciate that so much. I appreciate *him* so much. My life is a fairytale because of him. I slipped into his bed and found that it fit me just right. *He* fit me just right. He's fit me just right every day since. My grumpy daddy bear is my world, and I'm his. I'm as obsessed with him as ever. I don't have to ask to know he feels the same. He shows me that every day.

When the kids go down at night, my beastly daddy comes out to play. He's as unruly as ever, unable to keep his hands off me. He fucks me like he can't stop, sometimes over and over again. And when I can't take anymore, he gets to have his fun. He pampers and spoils me like a true princess. In those moments, I'm the most cherished little princess in the world. And he's the most satisfied daddy on the planet.

We have to tone it down around the kids, but even then, he always makes a point to take care of me. He makes sure I know that I'm his little princess. Most days, I eat on his lap. He carries me around, cooks for me, and spoils me rotten. Not a day goes by when he doesn't take time to hold me and our babies. We are so loved.

I think most of his brothers know about the dynamics of our relationship at this point, but no one judges us. They simply accept us for who we are. The wives do too. Truthfully, I think a few of the brothers are a little kinky too. Women talk! I know way more about their sex lives than I ever needed to know. But I love them all so much! They are the sisters I never had.

Dimitri is married now too. His wife is amazing. I adore her so much. She's shy and sweet and perfect for Dimitri. He treats her like a queen. I love seeing him so happy. It's all I've ever wanted for him. Even Uncle Dante and Constantine found love in Silver Spoon Falls. I never thought I'd see the day my uncle fell in love, but he fell like a ton of bricks.

Life looks a lot different now than it did five years ago. It's bigger, brighter, and so much fuller. I love every moment of it. Especially the ones when my family is all together. Nothing makes me happier than having all the people I love in the same place.

"Are we going in, mommy?" Dylan asks, tugging on the hem of my shirt.

"Yep," I whisper. "But you have to be quiet as a mouse so we don't wake him up or we'll ruin the surprise, remember?"

"I a'member," she says, rolling her little blue eyes like I'm annoying her. I swear she does not get that from me. Jude says she does, but I think he's crazy. She lifts her little arms, impatient for me to pick her up to help her climb through the window.

I haul her up over my pregnant belly, saying a pray that Jude is still asleep. If he wakes up with me climbing through his window, he's going to spank me. Which is kind of the point, but I'd prefer to enjoy my punishment later and not get the lecture I know I'll get if he actually catches me crawling through the window. He's so bossy! Every time I get pregnant, he gets extra protective.

I don't really mind, but I'm not very good at following the rules either. The truth is...I like it when my grumpy daddy bear comes out to play. His punishments are my favorite. Finding ways to earn them is one of my favorite things to do.

I never put myself in harm's way, but Jude thinks anything more than walking across a flat surface is the equivalent of skydiving. Considering that he had steps installed under his window the first time I crawled through when I was pregnant with Dylan, I think I'm pretty safe here. He would beg to differ. So I misbehave to remind him that he is not the boss of me, as much as he likes to think he is.

I help Dylan onto the steps and then clamber onto the bottom one to peer through the window. Jude is passed out in the bed, one arm thrown over his eyes. My stomach flutters when I see his bare chest. His leg is bent at an angle, pulling the sheets down to reveal that he's wearing boxers. Thank goodness. Dylan does not need to see what is underneath them. She already asks a million questions a day.

"It's daddy!" she says, bouncing excitedly. "Look, mommy! Him is here!"

"I know, baby girl," I whisper. "You gotta be quiet."

"Oh, yeah," she says.

I wait for a second to make sure Jude isn't going to wake up and then slowly slide the window open. Dylan shifts impatiently, eager to get inside. She is a daddy's girl through and through. She loves nothing more than to curl up and make Jude read to her. She never wants to read princess books either. Oh no.

She wants stories about knights and dragons and danger.

She's either going to burn the world to the ground one day...or run for president. Either one is equally possible. She's a fierce little girl with fierce opinions. I can't wait to see what she becomes when she's older. The world probably trembled in fear the day she was born. I love her so much!

Her little brothers are a lot more chill than she is. Duke is three and Dawson is two. They're both tame little boys. They follow Dylan around, marching to her orders. They're protective of her though. A little boy pushed her on the playground last month. Duke tried to spank him. Dawson bit him. They nearly started a riot. We all left in tears. We're never going back to that playground again.

"Careful," I whisper, lifting Dylan up over the windowsill. She grabs onto the ledge and plops down before wiggling forward. Within seconds, she's standing on her feet on the other side, beaming at me.

"Your turn, mommy," she whispers...mostly.

I pull myself up the steps and then squeeze through the frame. It's a lot easier when I'm not six months pregnant. Eventually, I manage to fit myself through, though. I step into Jude's room, slightly out of breath and only a little sweaty.

"What are you doing?"

"Ahh!" I scream, jumping a foot into the air. I spin around to see Jude standing behind me, holding Dylan in his arms.

"Daddy's awake," she says. The little traitor.

"I see that," I say, and then scowl at him. "You scared the crap out of me."

"Yeah?" He smirks, leaning down to kiss me. "That wouldn't be a problem if you'd use the fucking door, princess."

"It could have been locked," I mumble against his lips.

"You have a key."

"It's at home."

"Why didn't you bring it?"

Because I had no intention of using it. Not that I'm telling him that.

"Forgot," I lie, cuddling up against his chest.

He snorts, not believing me for a minute. He never does. I swear he always knows when I'm lying. He has those ridiculous lawyer spidey senses. They can smell my bullshit a mile away. At least that's what I tell myself. I refuse to believe it's because I'm a terrible liar.

"We sneaked in to surpwise you, daddy," Dylan says.

Well, crap.

"Are you surpwised?"

"Very," Jude says somberly.

I'm so busted.

"Yay!" Dylan cheers.

"Why don't you go see what Aunt Gloria has in the kitchen for you, baby girl?" he says. "I bet she has cookies with your name on them."

"Oh, cookies!" Dylan whispers, wiggling in his arms to get down. Of course she whispers this time. Nothing speaks to her heart quite like chocolate.

Jude carries her to the door, unlocking it before he sets her on her feet. She immediately takes off, skipping down the hall. He shouts to Gloria to let her know that Dylan is coming out and then waits for Gloria to shout back before closing the door. The lock clicks into place, making my belly flip.

"Are you wearing panties under that pretty dress, princess?" he asks, leaning up against the door. His blue eyes rake over me, hot and wild.

"Yes."

"Lose them."

My pulse skitters off beat.

"Now."

I immediately reach beneath my dress, tugging them down my legs and then stepping out of them. They're already damp. I'm already soaked. That's no surprise. All he has to do is look at me and I'm wet.

"Hands on the desk," he growls. "Ass in the air."

I moan softly, scurrying to obey. My breath rasps in my throat, my heart pounding against my breastbone. I feel his eyes on me, but he doesn't move yet.

He makes me wait. Lets the anticipation build until I'm squirming.

"You've been misbehaving again, princess," he says, stalking toward me.

"I'm sorry, daddy," I whimper.

"Are you?"

"No."

His hand curves around my hip, pulling my dress up. "Didn't think so," he says, chuckling. "That's why daddy has to punish you, princess."

"Daddy," I whine. The cool air in the room brushes across my ass, followed by the palm of his hand. I writhe in anticipation.

"Good girls don't crawl through their daddy's windows, princess," he growls.

"No," I gasp. "The best girls do."

"Fuck." His hand comes down on my ass in a sharp smack.

I bite my lip to stifle my cry of pleasure.

He swats my other cheek and then shoves his hand between my legs to play with me. "You drive your daddy crazy, princess," he says, biting the shell of my ear. "I can't fucking resist you when you say things like that and you know it."

"You love it," I moan, rocking back against his hand.

"God, yeah, I do."

"I needed you, daddy."

"You missed me?"

"So bad," I sob.

"You need your daddy's cock, princess?"

"Yes!"

I don't have to say it twice. The next thing I know, he's inside me, yanking me back on his cock. I can't quiet my cry this time. I shout his name into the room, already so close to the edge. With him, it doesn't take much to get me there.

He covers my mouth with his hand to keep me quiet, fucking me hard and deep. His grunts and soft curses are my favorite song. I rock back against him, taking him to the hilt again and again. It's quick and dirty and still so full of love.

"Soak daddy's dick, baby doll," he growls in my ear. "Get it nice and sloppy so you can lick it clean later like the best little girls do."

I cry out against his hand, my inner muscles clamping down on him.

"Yeah, I knew you'd like that, princess."

I do. God help me, I do.

"Come with me," he whispers, nuzzling his face into my throat. "Give it to daddy."

My body bows over the desk as my orgasm hits, waves crashing through me. They submerge me completely, drowning me in bliss. In him. I let them carry me away, floating in ecstasy as he grunts my name and then stills, spilling into me.

"I love you," he whispers when it's over, his lips at my ear.

"I love you too, daddy." I groan, trying to stand upright, but my legs are all wobbly.

"Steady, baby doll," he says. "Let me clean you up."

I wait patiently for him to clean me up, only to groan when I see him carrying my panties toward me. "Daddy," I protest, even as my stomach quivers in delight.

He arches a brow. "You know the punishment for lying to me, princess," he says. "You'll wear your wet panties to remind you that good girls tell their daddies the truth."

"Yes, daddy," I whisper.

He cleans me up with my panties and then helps me step into them, pulling them up my legs. They're soaked with my juices and his cum. Which is exactly what he likes. I'll never tell him, but so do I. Pretending I don't is part of our game.

"Come here," he says, pulling me into his arms.

I snuggle in with a happy sigh.

"You gotta stop crawling through the window, baby doll," he says, rubbing my belly. "My little girl is in here."

"Your little girl is the reason I almost didn't fit through the window this time," I pout.

"You're perfect, Devin," he growls. "Don't you ever think otherwise."

"Okay," I agree, knowing he means it. In his eyes, I am perfect. It's hard to be upset about getting bigger when he looks at me like I'm pure magic the whole time I'm pregnant. I don't have to ask to know he thinks I'm beautiful. It's written all over his face.

"Are you sleepy, baby doll?"

"A little bit," I say.

"Why don't you nap for a little while?" He scoops me up into his arms, carrying me across to the bed. "I'll watch Dylan until your brother gets here with the boys."

"Are you sure?" I run my hands through his hair. "Aren't you tired?" He's the one who drove to Houston well before dawn just so he could drive back to be here in time for the party today. It's Cash's birthday. He didn't want to miss it. He wanted to come back to the house, but I convinced him to come here instead so he could get some sleep. It made more sense than making him get up even earlier to get ready to come here.

"I'm good, princess," he promises, depositing me in the bed. "I slept for a couple of hours." He brushes my hair back from my face, smiling at me. "And I got inside my princess. That's all I need to keep going."

"Daddy," I whisper.

"Rest, baby doll," he says, leaning forward to kiss me. "You're going to need it for later. Your daddy has plans for you."

"Oh, yeah?" I wrap my arms around his neck, pulling him down for another kiss. "What kind of plans?"

"The kind that'd have you pregnant with my kid if you weren't already so swollen with my baby that the whole fucking world knows daddy can't keep his dick out of you," he growls, nipping at my bottom lip.

I groan softly, suddenly wide awake.

Jude notices and chuckles.

"It's daddy's turn to take care of you now, baby doll," he says, running the back of his hand down the side of my face. "Sleep."

"I love you," I whisper, obediently closing my eyes.

His warm breath washes across my face in a gentle sigh. "I love you with everything I have, princess. Always."

I snuggle in and drift off, safe and warm in his bed.

AUTHOR'S NOTE

I f you enjoyed The Lawyer, please consider leaving a review! I appreciate them so much!

Are you ready to take a wild ride with the Silver Spoon MC series? The next book in the series, The Architect by Loni Ree, releases August 5th!

Next up from me is Beach House Beauty, my addition to the Rental Rendezvous series, releasing July 25th!

SILVER SPOON MC

These wealthy Texans have it all—Money, looks, power, their MC, and brothers. The only thing missing is someone to share it all with. There's a shortage of eligible ladies in town but these determined men won't let that slow them down. These MC brothers are going to turn the town of Silver Spoon Falls, Texas, on its ear looking for their curvy soulmates.

Beginning in February 2022, Nichole Rose and Loni Ree are bringing you the Silver Spoon MC Series and these aren't your typical MC romance stories. Nichole and Loni like to keep things light. Come along with us on this wild instalove ride.

The CEO by Loni Ree - February 4, 2022

http://mybook.to/TheCEOLoniRee

The Surgeon by Nichole Rose - March 1, 2022

http://mybook.to/TheSurgeon

The Cowboy by Loni Ree - April 4, 2022 -

https://books2read.com/TheCowboyLoniRee

The Heir by Nichole Rose - May 3, 2022 -

http://mybook.to/TheHeirNR

The Rockstar by Loni Ree - June 10, 2022

https://books2read.com/TheRockstar

The Lawyer by Nichole Rose - July 5, 2022

http://mybook.to/TheLawyerNR

The Architect by Loni Ree- August 5, 2022

books2read.com/TheArchitectLoniRee

The Prodigy by Nichole Rose- September 6, 2022

http://mybook.to/TheProdigyNR

The Prince by Loni Ree - October 7, 2022

https://books2read.com/ThePrinceLoniRee

The Bodyguard by Nichole Rose- November 1, 2022

http://mybook.to/TheBodyguardNR

Instalove Book Club

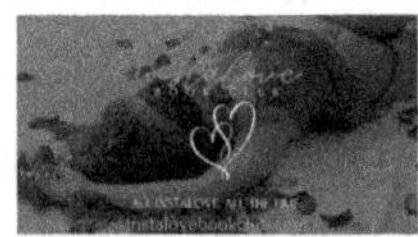

The Instalove Book Club is now in session!

Get the inside scoop from your favorite instalove authors, meet new authors to love, and snag freebies and bonus content from featured authors every month. The Instalove Book Club newsletter goes out once per week!

Join now to get your hands on bonus scenes and brand-new, exclusive content from our first six featured authors.

Join the Club: http://instaloveinstalovebookclub.com

Beach House Beauty

EXCERPT

A heavy silence permeates the bar. The only sound is the blood rushing in a thick hum through my veins and the final, mournful strains of my song as it fades to a whisper. My chest barely rises, my breaths shallow. I keep my eyes closed, waiting for the final note of the song to fade.

I feel Rhys watching me from the shadows, his gaze heavy. It sets me on fire, making me ache for him. Always, I ache for him.

I take another shallow breath and release it. It seems unnaturally loud in the deafening silence around me.

No one moves.

Five seconds tick by.

Ten.

Fifteen.

Thunderous applause erupts from every corner of the room, as deafening as the silence that preceded it. Triumph blooms in my chest, relief. I poured my whole soul into that song, and they loved it.

I spin and rush off the stage, eager to get to Rhys, to share this moment with him.

As soon as he sees me coming toward him, he opens his arms, ready to catch me. I crash into him like a meteor, knocking him back a little deeper into the shadows. His body engulfs me, his breathing ragged. His erection presses against my belly. All I see in the dark are his green eyes blazing with unholy fire.

"Goddamn, Raven," he growls.

Our lips meet, our tongues moving in a perfectly choreographed dance. We melt into one another, a tangle of trembling limbs and greedy desperation. Of forbidden desire and helpless addiction. We're slaves to it, unable to deny the strength of the bond between us.

He's my father's best friend, but that's not what I'm thinking about when he touches me. All I think about is how good he is to me, and how badly I ache for him. All I see is him, that big body hewn from one thick slab of muscle. Those tattoos painted across his golden-brown skin. The angular cut of his jaw and the full, uneven lips that kiss me like he plans to survive off me.

"You sing like a fucking angel," he whispers, breaking the kiss to look at me. His expression is aswirl with emotion. Pride. Possession. Desire.

Does he know I sang for him? That I meant every word?

"I missed you," I whisper instead of telling him.

"Yeah?" he asks.

I bob my head, strands of my hair catching on the wooden wall. We're completely hidden from the rest of the bar, tucked in an alcove behind the stage. They're only yards away, but miles might as well separate us. They're muted, their applause fading as the owner of the island bar introduces the next act for the night.

"Were you singing for me, sweet Raven?" Rhys asks, his firm hands locking down on my hips.

"I..."

"Don't lie to me, little girl."

"Yes," I whisper.

He grunts his satisfaction, pulling me closer. I feel the hard ridge of his erection against my belly. Anticipation turns my nipples to hard points. We're in the middle of a bar, and I want him anyway. I think some part of me wants him right now *because* we're in the middle of a bar. There's a naughty, forbidden edge to the desire coursing through my veins. I know he won't allow anyone to see me. But the thought that they're so close...I like it.

"Rhys? I need you."

A growl rumbles in his throat.

"Please," I whisper, feeling like I might spiral out of control. I've never thought about having sex like this, with one hundred other people so close. But I'm not surprised. When Rhys touches me, nothing else matters. He consumes me, turns me into some wanton version of myself that I find myself eager to know. She's braver than I am, bolder. Capable of keeping this dark prince worshipping at her feet.

"You need to come, Raven?" he asks, spinning me around in his arms so I'm staring out at the stage. His hand splays across my belly, so low I feel the heat of it between my legs. "You want me inside you right here?"

I moan his name.

"Tell me," he demands, pressing his lips to my exposed shoulder. His hand creeps lower.

Warmth rushes through me, every nerve ending in my body firing.

"Tell me, Raven."

"Yes." The word is a mere whisper of sound exhaled into the shadows.

"No, princess. I want you to say the words. Open that sweet mouth and tell me what you want me to do to you."

Beach House Beauty releases July 25th.

FOLLOW NICHOLE

Sign-up for Nichole's mailing list at http://authorn icholerose.com/newsletter to stay up to date on all new releases and for exclusive ARC giveaways from Nichole Rose.

Want to connect with Nichole and other readers? Join Nichole Rose's Book Beauties on Facebook!

f

facebook.com/AuthorNicholeRose/

instagram.com/AuthorNicholeRose

twitter.com/AuthNicholeRose

bookbub.com/authors/nichole-rose

tiktok.com/@authornicholerose

MORE BY NICHOLE ROSE

<u>Her Alpha Series</u>
Her Alpha Daddy Next Door
Her Alpha Boss Undercover
Her Alpha's Secret Baby
Her Alpha Protector
Her Date with an Alpha
Her Alpha: The Complete Series

<u>Her Bride Series</u>
His Future Bride
His Stolen Bride
His Secret Bride
His Curvy Bride
His Captive Bride
His Blushing Bride
His Bride: The Complete Series

Claimed Series
Possessing Liberty
Teaching Rowan
Claiming Caroline
Kissing Kennedy
Claimed: The Complete Series

Love on the Clock Series
Adore You
Hold You
Keep You
Protect You
Love on the Clock: The Complete Series

The Billionaires' Club
The Billionaire's Big Bold Weakness
The Billionaire's Big Bold Wish
The Billionaire's Big Bold Woman
The Billionaire's Big Bold Wonder

Playing for Keeps
Cutie Pie
Ice Breaker
Ice Prince
Ice Giant (coming soon)

<u>The Second Generation</u>
A Blushing Bride for Christmas

Love Bites
Come Undone
Dripping Pearls

<u>Silver Spoon MC</u>
The Surgeon
The Heir
The Lawyer
The Prodigy
The Bodyguard

<u>Echoes of Forever</u>
His Christmas Miracle
Taken by the Hitman
Wicked Saint

<u>The Ruined Trilogy</u>
Physical Science
Wrecked

Destination Romance
Romancing the Cowboy
Beach House Beauty

Standalone Titles
A Touch of Summer
Black Velvet
His Secret Obsession
Dirty Boy
Naughty Little Elf
Devil's Deceit
A Bride for the Beast (writing with Fern Fraser)

Easy on Me
Easy Ride
Easy Surrender

One Night with You
Falling Hard
Model Behavior
Learning Curve
Angel Kisses

writing with Loni Ree as Loni Nichole

Dillon's Heart
Razor's Flame
Ryker's Reward (coming soon)
Zane's Rebel (coming soon)

ABOUT NICHOLE ROSE

Nichole Rose is a short romance author on the west coast. Her books feature headstrong, sassy women and the alpha males who consume them. From grumpy detectives to country boys with attitude to instalove and over-the-top declarations, nothing is off-limits.

Nichole is sure to have a steamy, sweet story just right for everyone. She fully believes the world is ugly enough without trying to fit falling in love into a one-size-fits-all box. When not writing, Nichole enjoys fine wine, cute shoes, and everything supernatural. She is happily married to the love of her life and is a proud mama to the world's most ridiculous fur-babies.

You can learn more about Nichole and her books at authornicholerose.com.

f

facebook.com/AuthorNicholeRose/

instagram.com/AuthorNicholeRose

twitter.com/AuthNicholeRose

BB

bookbub.com/authors/nichole-rose

tiktok.com/@authornicholerose